Loving Lucianna

Other works by Joyce DiPastena

Poitevin Hearts series

Illuminations of the Heart (Poitevin Hearts 2)
Loving Lucianna (Poitevin Hearts 3)
Dangerous Favor (Poitevin Hearts 4)

Additional Titles

Courting Cassandry
The Lady and the Minstrel
An Epiphany Gift for Robin: A short prequel scene to The Lady and the Minstrel (free on Amazon)
The Girl by the River: A short prequel scene to The Lady and the Minstrel (free on Amazon)
A Candlelight Courting
"Caroles on the Green," in *Timeless Romance Anthology: Winter Edition*

Non-fiction

Name Your Medieval Character: Medieval Christian Names (12th-13th Centuries)

A POITEVIN
HEARTS
ROMANCE

Loving Lucianna

JOYCE DiPASTENA

Sable Tyger Books

Janet e Joyce, sorelle sempre

Cast of Characters

Characters (in alphabetical order)

Acelet de Cary: cousin of Triston de Brielle (appeared in *Illuminations of the Heart*)

Alessandro de Calendri: Siri's first husband; deceased (mentioned in *Illuminations of the Heart*)

Antonia d'Arro Amorosi: wife of Domenico Amorosi; mother of Serafino Amorosi

Balduin de Soler: a knight in the household of Triston de Brielle (introduced in *Illuminations of the Heart*)

Domenico Amorosi: a woolmonger in Venice; husband of Antonia d'Arro Amorosi; father of Serafino Amorosi

Elisabetta Gallo Geraud: Siri's mother; deceased (mentioned in *Illuminations of the Heart*)

Folcaut (mentioned): a troubadour at Duke Richard's court

Giovanni: a servant in the household of Domenico and Antonia Amorosi

Jaufre (mentioned): a troubadour at Duke Richard's court

Lisette: a young girl in the court of Duke Richard of Aquitaine (introduced in *Illuminations of the Heart*)

Lucianna Fabio: friend of Elisabetta Gallo Geraud; companion of Siri de Brielle (introduced in *Illuminations of the Heart*)

Maria Angela: a nun at the Convent of Saint Catherine (*convento de Santa Caterina*)

Perrin de Brielle: Triston's son by his first wife (appears in *Loyalty's Web* and *Illuminations of the Heart*)

Richard, Duke of Aquitaine: second son of King Henry II of England and Queen Eleanor of Aquitaine (appears in *Loyalty's Web* and *Illuminations of the Heart*)

Mother Rosalba: abbess of the Convent of Saint Catherine (*convento de Santa Caterina*)

Serafino Amorosi: a woolmonger from Venice; son of Domenico and Antonia Amorosi

Simon Geraud: Siri's brother; deceased (mentioned in *Illuminations of the Heart*)

Siri de Brielle: wife of Triston de Brielle; step-mother of Perrin de Brielle (heroine of *Illuminations of the Heart*)

Triston de Brielle: lord of Vere Castle; husband of Siri de Brielle; father of Perrin de Brielle (introduced in *Loyalty's Web*; hero of *Illuminations of the Heart*)

Vincenzo Mirolli: a young merchant's son in Venice

Walter Geraud: Siri's father; deceased (mentioned in *Illuminations of the Heart*)

1

Convento di Santa Caterina ~ Venice 1147

She could not work with so much wailing in her ears! Lucianna hooked her small bone needle in the cloth. She had been forbidden the long, graceful needles of bronze the nuns used until her hands grew larger. They said in their scolding voices that she must be patient for that should be a very long time, for she was only nine years old. She exuded a huff. She did not like being patient. And she did not like the girl who had been thrust into the dormitory she shared with Sister Maria Angela in the almonry. Elisabetta, they called her. She had done nothing but weep from the day she had arrived.

The wailings drifted through the dormitory window, assaulting Lucianna's ears where she sat on a bench outside beneath one of the many olive trees the nuns harvested for oil. How could one stitch a decent flower with so much racket in one's brain? Lucianna folded the linen very neatly, as she had been taught to do, set it reverently in the small workbasket at her feet, rose from the bench, smoothed the creases from the skirts of her humble russet gown, bade farewell to the lovely spring morning she had been enjoying, and went inside to do the duty that had been assigned to her.

She had been asked by the abbess to comfort the frightened, lonely girl. Lucianna had been lonely, too, the only child in the convent, though Sister Maria Angela said there had been oblates before her and would certainly be oblates donated to the abbey again. But none had come in Lucianna's nine years, until a fortnight ago. She had *thought, perhaps, she and Elisabetta might become friends but the endless laments had finally exhausted her patience.*

"Why do you weep like this?" she said crossly to the girl sprawled sobbing on the narrow bed beside her own. "If I behaved so unseemly, Sister Maria Angela would take her switch to me. But you are coddled and given warm blankets and allowed to wear those pretty gowns your father sent with you." She dared not confess her envy of the gowns, especially that green one that would have matched her eyes. "And one day you shall go back home to the father who loves you. So why do you cry and cry and cry?"

Elisabetta sat up. Her dark hair with the reddish highlights that peeped out when she sat in the sun now fell tangled over her tear stained face. "I hate it here!" she said. "I miss my own wide bed and the gingerbread from our kitchens and my father's pretty rose garden — "

"You are spoiled."

"And most of all I miss my father, for he would never let you speak to me that way!"

Lucianna shrugged. Sister Maria Angela would switch her if she saw it, but the nun was working in the herb garden. Sometimes they made Lucianna work there as well, but her gift for embroidering delicate designs had so pleased the abbess, that most days she was allowed to sit on the bench outside the dormitory window and practice her stitching instead. One day, when her talent had matured, her work would be sold and the money given as alms to the poor.

"Do you think if you cry enough your father will take you away sooner?" Lucianna asked, barely concealing her scorn. Or perhaps it was jealousy. No one would ever come to take her away, no matter how hard she wished it.

Elisabetta dried her eyes with a soft silken sleeve woven with yellow birds, and shook her head.

"Then what good does it do you to weep like this?" Lucianna sat down on her own bed. She wondered what silk would feel like against her skin. As long as she could remember, the nuns had dressed her in rough woven russet. She ran her fingers over her skirts as she waited for an answer.

12

"I cannot help it," Elisabetta said. "I try to be brave, but it is so horrid here. Do you not hate it, too?"

"I have never known any place but this. My parents died when I was a baby and left me to the nuns."

Elisabetta's dark brown eyes went wide. "Oh, but that is sad!"

Lucianna knew better than to indulge in pity for herself. It changed nothing and only brought down Sister Maria Angela's condemnation upon her head.

"My father's name was Panfilo," Lucianna said. "My mother — I do not know. I call her Rosaria, but I do not know if that was her name. I think it is pretty, though."

She plucked at a loose thread on her skirts. It would make a hole if she tugged at it, but she pulled it anyway. Sister Maria Angela would make her mend the rent it caused. Anything was better than working in the herb garden where the thorns pricked her fingers. The last time they had done so, she had not been able to embroider for days.

"You are lucky," she said, wiggling a finger through the hole she had made in her gown.

"Lucky?" Elisabetta stared as though Lucianna had stood too long beneath the moon. "To sleep in a cold bed at night and eat dried beans and crumbling cheese and black bread instead of gingerbread? To be made to sit for hours in silence while they read psalms at you or kneel until your knees are raw from prayer?"

"They excuse us from the night office because we are young. And it is much colder in the winter than it is now in the spring. You will not be here forever and ever, like I will. And you have a warm blanket to sleep in at night."

And a gown that would make my eyes shine like the emerald clasp on the mantle of the lady who stayed with her servants one night in the guest house last year.

Lucianna's parents had left her a red brooch in a silver setting, but the nuns would not let her wear it for fear she should become vain. She tried not to mind. Besides, it went ill with her auburn hair.

"It is not as quiet now as it was before you came." Lucianna pulled at another thread. The hole in her skirt grew wider. "Before, the nuns only spoke when they read the psalms or prayed and when they scolded me because I do not like to clean or cook or work in the herb garden, and I do not like to sit still, unless I am stitching a pattern. But now you wail and wail and they never scold you. They speak meekly and caressingly to you, then tell me I must comfort you when your tears do not cease."

Elisabetta drew up her knees on the bed and wrapped her arms around them. "You have not tried to comfort me at all!"

"Well, it is hard when you are so ungrateful. No one asks you to cook or clean or garden, but to learn how to read and to write and to count and speak French. Why does your father wish you to learn all those things?"

Another tear rolled down Elisabetta's cheek, but this time silently. Again she wiped it away with her sleeve. "After my mother died, my father said he had not time to take care of me. I think it was because it made him too sad to think of Mama. He said one day I should make a very great marriage, because he said I should have great beauty when I am older and he will provide me with a dowry to tempt a great lord. But if the lords should spurn me and I marry a merchant like himself instead, then it will be a help to my husband for me to read and write and count."

"And the French?" Lucianna wrinkled her nose. Why should any woman of Venice need to speak French?

"My father trades with men of many lands and some of them are French. So he wishes me to learn, that I might help my husband, should my husband be a merchant. But if he is a lord, then I need only know how to be pretty and embroider. I hate embroidery."

Lucianna glowered, as though an insult had been hurled at her. How could anyone hate the brightly colored skeins of silk, or the smooth flow of the threads as one drew them through the cloth? It was the only time Lucianna felt quiet inside.

"I cannot comfort someone as silly as you," she declared and bounced up from her bed.

"Wait!" Elisabetta called as Lucianna started down the long line of empty beds towards the door.

Lucianna had no choice as Sister Maria Angela came in just

14

then. Dirt stained the nun's habit and as always, her nails were blackened with soil from the garden. Lucianna hid her own hands behind her back. She could not bear filthy nails and was always picking at her own to keep them clean. Sister Maria Angela had switched her for it more than once, calling Lucianna prideful. Impatience and pride were sins the abbess agreed must be stripped from Lucianna before she grew old enough to take her vows.

But now Sister Maria Angela beamed a smile. Lucianna had not known the nun knew how to smile before Elisabetta came. As always, the pleasant expression was turned on the dark haired girl whom the nuns always called their "guest."

"You are not crying." Approval rang in Sister Maria Angela's voice. "Then we will resume your French instruction. Come with me to the chapel."

Elisabetta's dark eyes widened and Lucianna saw something in them she had never seen before, perhaps because they were usually buried against the bolster in tears. Fear. Lucianna was not sure how she knew it, but something whispered to her, See! It is what you feel when Sister Maria Angela brings out her switch. *Surely the nun had never taken her slender birch rod to the back of Elisabetta's legs?*

No, but Elisabetta has seen Sister Maria Angela switch me here in the dormitory.

And sometimes the switch struck higher than Lucianna's legs. Was that why Elisabetta did not wish to be alone while the nun instructed her? Is that why she wept and wept and wept?

Lucianna started as Sister Maria Angela laid her hand atop Lucianna's head. She tried not to cringe from the soil-crusted fingers.

"Well done, my child. I knew you would not fail us."

She did not smile at Lucianna, but approval rang in her tones. Did she think Lucianna had finally found a way to quiet Elisabetta's tears?

Elisabetta slid slowly from the bed, eying the nun with dread as she trailed her slowly towards the door. But when she came abreast of Lucianna, she suddenly slid their hands together, tightly lacing their fingers.

15

"May she come with me," Elisabetta said in a trembling voice, "and sit with me while you teach me?"

Sister Maria Angela's mouth turned sternly downward. "Lucianna came to this house with no dowry save for a single brooch. We will sell it when she comes of age for her vows. Then she will pray and sing when the bells are rung, she will take her turn in the kitchen and garden, she will spin cloth, and because she has a gift, she will embroider. But she is not to be among our number who learns to read and she will never have use for numbers, still less to ever speak French."

To Lucianna's surprise, Elisabetta tossed her dark head and jutted her chin into the air with a stubbornness that for the first time hinted of a kindred spirit. "Then I shall stay here and weep for my father and my home. I do not want to sit alone with you. It is dull and you will switch me if I misspeak a word."

"Of course I will not," Sister Maria Angela said indignantly. "Your father paid us generously to treat you well."

Lucianna set her lips close to Elisabetta's ear and hissed, "I do not wish to speak French."

Elisabetta whispered back, "I will let you teach me to embroider if you come, and I will not weep anymore. I promise." Then she repeated very loudly, "I will only come if Lucianna may come, too."

No more sobbing through the night? No more wailings to disturb Lucianna with her needle? It would be worth enduring all the pointless lessons if it made Elisabetta quiet. And Lucianna imagined she might enjoy instructing the other girl in the embroidery she so loved.

Sister Maria Angela heaved a loud, exasperated sigh. "Very well, Lucianna may sit with you. But she may not speak, write, or count numbers. Do you understand?"

Lucianna breathed a breath of relief at this promise. Her mind filled with blissful visions of teaching Elisabetta how to stitch, she nodded with the other girl, then hands still locked together, they followed the nun out of the dormitory.

One

⁓

Poitou ~ Autumn 1180

Lucianna's heart fluttered as Sir Balduin de Soler's fingers brushed against hers. She was certain the gesture was deliberate, although his deeply tanned hand moved quickly and smoothly past hers to touch the snow white silk she had selected. He nodded his approval, though she suspected he had never bought an ell of cloth in his life and scarce knew the difference between cendal and samite. She guessed from the small smile at the corners of his mouth that his gesture, like his offer to accompany her to this market town, had merely been an excuse to indulge his affection for her. Lucianna had been much abustle the last few weeks with little time for him, hovering over the young woman she had mothered for so many years, who would soon be a mother of her own.

Lucianna had inspected every bolt of cloth in the clothier's shop before settling on the samite. Only one fabric in the shop was more costly—baudekin, the clothier called it, a delicate brocade with airily graceful figures woven into a pale gold background. But gold would not do for a babe's baptismal gown. That required the purest white. Lucianna intended to decorate the cloth with elaborate embroidery—

also white, of course — for nothing could be too beautiful for Siri's firstborn child.

Lucianna blinked away the sting of a tear. It seemed only yesterday that she had sat at the bedside of Siri's mother, cradling her wee little daughter in her arms while Elisabetta slept. How the years had flown! Elisabetta gone, Siri grown, married, widowed, and now wed again so very happily to Lord Triston de Brielle of Vere Castle. And expecting her first child in a mere two months.

Sir Balduin's other hand found the small of Lucianna's back and rested there with a familiar intimacy, as though sensing her need for comfort through her sudden burst of nostalgia.

"And how does the lad Perrin go on?" the stocky, grey-haired clothier inquired of Sir Balduin after asking about the health of the lord of Vere Castle and his wife.

"He's grown into a clever boy," Sir Balduin replied, "though sometimes a bit too precocious for his own good. Lord Triston has him learning Latin among many other things. Perrin will not stand heir to the barony as those lands came to Lord Triston through his marriage to the Lady Siri. Perrin will inherit only Vere, so I do not know what use Latin will be to him." Sir Balduin gave a small shrug without removing his hand from her back, a tacit embrace that had begun to radiate as much possessiveness as comfort. "But Lord Triston is determined to educate the lad as thoroughly as any monk . . . perhaps because he wishes his father had allowed him to learn such knowledge himself when he was a boy."

Lucianna only half-listened as the two men discussed Siri's stepson. Sir Balduin, at fifty-two, had known the twenty-eight-year-old Triston all his life. He had shared with Lucianna some of the young man's struggles and troubles that Sir Balduin had witnessed while he stood as a knight in service to Triston's late father, including the dark period of time after Perrin's birth when the clothier had briefly fostered him. She saw the way the door in the back of the workshop stood ajar and guessed that the clothier's plump, rosy-cheeked

18

wife was listening to every word. No doubt they hungered for news of the child they had once cared for, but to Lucianna it was all a distant story from the ancient past, events that had occurred before she and Siri had traveled here from Venice.

Only their past year in Poitou felt immediate and still vivid to Lucianna: Siri's brother's will that had sent her from their home to the guardianship of the widowed Triston de Brielle; the turbulent courtship that had followed between Siri and the impulsive, hot-tempered Triston; and the grey-haired knight with the surprisingly whimsical smiles who had wooed Lucianna and won her heart when he had so bravely defended Lucianna's precious, beautiful charge, Elisabetta's daughter, in the nave of a cathedral when a lustful baron sought to abscond with Siri before she had married Triston.

Lucianna traced a series of patterns against the silk as the two men talked, already imagining the designs she would stitch there, but even while she did so she remained vitally aware of the man beside her. Sir Balduin stood half a head taller than the clothier, as strongly athletic despite a limp won in battle as the clothier tended to the portly. Where the clothier's grey hair thinned on top, Sir Balduin's remained thick with a handsome ripple in the back. Sir Balduin paused in his discourse on Perrin's education to "accidentally" brush Lucianna's hand again as he pointed to the spot in the cloth where her finger had idled.

"A rose there, don't you think, my love? No one stitches more elegant petals than you."

His hand nonchalantly grazed hers again as it withdrew, but not without a swift glance from his grey eyes that warmed her with its passion before he returned with his usual public composure to continue his conversation with the clothier.

Having seen Siri happily settled with Triston, Lucianna might have returned to Venice had it not been for Sir Balduin. At forty-four, she had been quite certain she was too old to fall in love. But Sir Balduin had been persistent from the first, sitting with her in the garden at Vere, praising her embroidery, asking her of Venice, telling her of her new home in Poitou, so clearly trying to find and build upon common interests between them. She had attempted to hold his advances at bay with the proud, haughty manners that had served her so well in Venice, but he had tempted her into the garden one balmy summer night and stolen a kiss that had nearly made her heart drum out of her breast. And then he had shown himself so brave when faced with the swords of a half-dozen knights commanded by the villainous baron, and comforted her so sweetly when she had feared Siri lost to the same. The next thing she had known, Triston had rescued Siri and the only thing lost had been Lucianna's heart to Sir Balduin. Now she wore his emerald ring on her finger and in less than in three weeks she would be his wife.

Her ears suddenly pricked at a word and she glanced up from the cloth to see Sir Balduin extending a handful of coins towards the clothier.

"What are you doing?" Lucianna exclaimed.

Sir Balduin looked startled. "Paying this good man for the cloth."

Lucianna mentally counted the coins and pronounced, "That is too much. Put the coins back in your purse, *signore*. I will deal with this 'good man.'" She drew some coins from her own purse, tied to the girdle she wore, and counted out half the number Sir Balduin had been about to offer.

"This will be quite sufficient," she told the clothier. "It is a fine cloth, *si*, but not nearly as fine as what I might purchase in Venice."

"But we are not in Venice," Sir Balduin said in that gentle voice he used whenever he sensed her feathers ruffled. She saw him cast a glance at the clothier and knew that the calm nature which so patiently bore with her caprices hoped to forestall the insult he appeared to think she had dealt the sturdy shopkeeper.

"Aye, we are not," the man agreed, "and the cost of transporting this silk all the way from your homeland must be factored into the price. I cannot part with it for less than your husband offered."

Lucianna's cheeks tingled with heat. "*Signor* Balduin is not my husband."

"Yet," Sir Balduin murmured with such a twinkle in his eye that Lucianna did not know whether to scold him or giggle. In truth, he made her blood rush as hot as it had at fifteen, coupled with a playfulness she had nearly forgotten she once possessed. When he smiled at her in just that way, he made her feel a mere girl again, before the silver wings in her auburn hair gazed back at her from her hand mirror every morn.

She endeavored to withstand the impulse to melt before his will. She would not be hoodwinked by a greedy clothier merely to please this knight who had brought joy to her lonely autumn soul with his smiles and his touch and his kisses.

"*Sta provando imbrogliarci*," Lucianna said with a frown at the clothier, before she threw a significant look at Sir Balduin.

Sir Balduin's mouth fell slightly open, even a the clothier demanded, "What did she say?"

It was not the surly tone in the shopkeeper's voice that snapped Lucianna's back so rigid that Sir Balduin's hand sprang away from it.

"*Imbrogliarci*," she repeated with an impatient tap of her toe. The blank look on Sir Balduin's face confirmed her suspicion. "You have not been attending to our lessons."

"I try," he insisted, with a defensiveness she had grown to recognize too well, "but most often they set my head spinning, especially when you speak the words so quickly. I do not see why I need to learn Italian in the first place. You speak French perfectly well."

"You said you would learn it to please me," she reminded him. "So that we can converse in my own language when I grow lonely for my home."

She watched the toe of his boot begin to beat a rhythm in tandem with hers against the boards of the floor. He rarely

21

showed impatience, but the Italian lessons invariably brought the uncommon emotion to the fore.

"You can converse with Lady Siri for that."

"And when we have moved to Dauvillier Castle? Who shall I talk to then? You promised—"

"And I am trying, but—"

She rolled her eyes towards the ceiling, exasperated with his protests. "It is perfectly simple. Say it slowly. *Sta pro-van-do im-bro-'liar-ci*. He-is-trying-to-cheat-us."

"I beg your pardon?" the clothier thundered so explosively that Lucianna jumped and Sir Balduin winced.

She did not know why the clothier should be offended. Haggling in Venice had always involved exchanges of "cheat" and "close-fisted parsimony," followed by a perfectly amicable accommodation in the end.

The clothier's plump wife came sailing out from behind the door at the back of the workshop, her round cheeks rosy with anger as she flew to her husband's defense. "Now see here! My husband is an honest man!"

Sir Balduin let loose a stream of swift, appeasing words, assuring them both that Lucianna had merely misspoken their own French tongue. Lucianna took exception to this, as she did to Sir Balduin's apparent intention of quieting the angry couple by pouring an outrageous number of coins into the clothier's palm in return for the silk. She would feign an apology to salvage Sir Balduin's embarrassment, but she would *not* allow the clothier to rob her beloved.

She had her hand half-extended towards Sir Balduin's sleeve to jerk back his hand with the coins when a tiny *plick* made her glance down to see a pebble bounce on the boards near her foot. She turned her head towards the only direction the small stone could have come from—the window.

Even in her most distraught moments as a young girl in Venice Lucianna had never been of a temperament to faint, but she came perilously close to doing so for the first time in her life when she saw the face in the window frame. The man did not need to crook a finger at her before his face disappeared to set her sweeping towards the exit of the shop.

"Lucianna?" Sir Balduin's voice halted her.

She racked her brain desperately for an excuse to escape. "I forgot the pins for Siri's hair. She asked me to buy her some pins. Ones with sapphires and diamonds—" Oh, heavens, she was babbling. As though Siri did not have dozens of sapphire and diamond studded pins for her hair! "I mean, she wished for"—Lucianna's gaze alighted on the ring on her finger—"she wished for a new emerald pin. Because she misplaced the one she brought with her from Venice."

Sir Balduin slipped the money into his purse and crossed the floor to wrap both hands about her shoulders. His frown held only worry now. Such tender worry that it set her eyes a-burn with tears.

"Sweetheart," he said softly, "are you quite well? Your cheeks are like chalk and you are—"

"Babbling, *si*, I know. It is only that I am cross with myself for having so nearly overlooked her request. I must go before I allow this *uomo avido* to provoke me into forgetting again."

The clothier's face went crimson, for in this instance her Italian was near enough to French for him to recognize himself being called a greedy man. She did not doubt that she outraged him further by turning her back on him and taking a swift step towards the door. Then she remembered who awaited her outside, turned back, untied her purse from her girdle and thrust it into Sir Balduin's hands.

"Pay him for the silk," she said curtly. "The gift is mine to Siri, so use my silver." She saw the rise of his brows and belatedly guessed his query. If she left him her money, how would she buy pins for Siri's hair? Her hands shaking slightly, she retrieved her purse, pulled out a few token coins, returned the purse to him and hurried out the door, calling over her shoulder, "Wait for me here. I will not be gone long.

The man with the dark auburn hair and vibrant green eyes said nothing as Lucianna grabbed the shabby brown sleeve of his tunic and dragged him around the side of the shop, far enough out of sight, she hoped, that no one passing by in the town would observe them conversing.

"What are you doing here?" she demanded. "How did you find me?"

The man grinned. "And I am overjoyed to see you, too, again, *cara*."

She flinched at the kiss he leaned forward to set on her cheek. Though ten years her senior, Nature had refrained from sullying his beauty with more than a faint web of lines at the corners of his eyes and a sprinkling of silver at the temples of his auburn hair, making his smooth, angelic features appear deceptively youthful and virtuous.

Panic set her heart hammering so hard she thought she might be ill. "But it is *impossibile* for you to have found me here!"

"Clearly not *impossibile*," he said, his French accented slightly stronger than her own. "*Infatti*, not even difficult. All your circle knew of Simon's will."

Siri's brother. With the last of their family gone in Venice, Simon had sent her at his death to their father's homeland of Poitou and the protection of the steadfast friend he had made on a pilgrimage, Triston de Brielle, all unaware of the unknown inheritance that awaited his sister here. Lucianna had not known how to warn Siri to tell no one of their destination without revealing the truth about Serafino. It had seemed too absurd that he would follow them all this way, so Lucianna had not bothered to try to concoct an excuse. But now, to her horror, here he was. How long had Serafino been in Poitou? Had the story of Siri's inheritance yet come to his ears?

"You have traveled a very long way for nothing," Lucianna attempted to feint. "This is not Venice. We live humbly here. I have nothing to give you."

Serafino's gaze glided from the top of her crisp white veil over her fine but simple blue linen gown to linger on the tips of her neat green shoes. At least she had had the good sense to abjure any of the rich surcotes she had brought with her from Venice so they would not be soiled by the dust of today's journey.

"More humble, indeed, than your days in Alessandro's house," Serafino agreed, referencing Siri's first husband, "yet you are not exactly in rags."

Lucianna struggled to wrestle down her alarm. "Go back. You are wasting your time here."

"I cannot go back, *cara*. I'm afraid I did something most foolish. I fell in love."

In spite of her agitation, Lucianna gave a disgusted snort. "Whose wife was it this time?"

She awaited his answer cynically. His grin could have charmed the birds from the heavens. What hope, then, that a lonely, neglected, and undoubtedly beautiful wife might resist him?

"*Don* Nicola Venanzio," he said without the least hint of shame. "Ah, but his wife was glorious! We had the most passionate *storia d'amore*. But even the best things must come to an end and at length I grew bored and careless. *Ahime! Don* Nicola proved a jealous and hot-blooded man who most crassly threatened to cut off my head when he learned what I had done." Serafino had the impudence to look indignant. "I thought it a jest at first, to salvage his injured pride, but he sent his guards after me and from the way they brandished their swords when they saw me, I decided it might be safest to take *Don* Nicola at his word. So I fled to Simon's workshop, certain you would lend me the means to visit Florence or Milano for a time, only when I got there I learned Simon had been dead for over a year and that his will had directed you to escort our lovely Siri to this faraway land they call Poitou."

Lucianna ignored the look of reproach he bent on her. He would have learned of Simon's death at the time had Serafino not been skulking in Ravenna as the result of an earlier *storia d'amore*, as he always termed his affairs. The hand mirror Lucianna had owned in Alessandro's house had paid his way that time. As always, Siri had replaced it when Lucianna pretended it had broken when Siri asked her where it had gone.

"I confess, I was quite cross with you at first," Serafino said. "But then I realized how the fates had smiled on me to send you away so that I would follow you and build a new life here at your side."

He smiled again that angelic smile that she had grown to hate.

"Jealous husbands cut off heads here in Poitou as well," she warned him. "But I am not without compassion for your plight. Here." She dropped the coins she had brought with her into his palm. "That will start you on your homeward journey. By the time you return to Venice, this *Don* Nicola will have forgotten all about you." The injured husbands always did eventually.

The smile faded as he studied her gift. "These will scarce carry me to the next town. A man must eat, you know, and pay for a place to sleep, and as you can see I am badly in need of a new tunic, plus there's the likelihood I should lose the rest of this on the roll of the dice, for how else is one to while away these dull autumn nights without a little gambling?"

He raised one auburn brow when her hand twitched. It would not have been the first time she slapped him in frustration, though the act never won more than a laugh from him—a laugh and a warning glint in his eye that always won her immediate capitulation to his demands. She balled her fingers into fists to prevent herself from succumbing to temptation. How could heaven be so cruel as to let him find her here?

Her motion drew Serafino's gaze to the emerald she wore.

"That ring now," Serafino said, "that could take me far. Did he give it to you, the man in the shop who gazed so adoringly at you even through his vexation when you offended the shopkeeper?"

Her mouth flooded with bitterness. She should have known

Serafino had been watching the entire scene, just as she should have thought to slip her ring into the purse she given Sir Balduin before she left the shop.

"You cannot have the ring," she said fiercely.

"I must have something."

"Not the ring." 'Twould be a sacrilege to bestow the gift of Sir Balduin's love on a scoundrel like Serafino.

Serafino did not look abashed by her vehemence. He raised a hand to stroke his clean-shaven chin—always a dangerous gesture. "I believe I should like to meet the man in the shop. I can sing your virtues to him. Do you still go by the name of Fabio, or—"

"*No!* Serafino, *no!*" All her defiance drained out of her, but she could not give him the ring. Her mind raced frantically. She must persuade him to go away, but if she offered too much he would come back again and again and again. She could not bear to relive that nightmare. "I have something else, that black silk gown that I embroidered in gold all over the bodice, the one you asked me to sell in Venice before I gave you my mirror instead. I brought it with me."

She tried not to remember how stunned with awe Sir Balduin had looked the first time he had seen her wear it, for she had known that it fired her auburn hair and made her skin shine white as milk. What would she say when he begged her to wear it again, as he frequently did? She gave her head a small shake. Better to explain away the gown than the ring.

"I will send you the gown before nightfall," she said. "Those coins I gave you will carry you to the next town and then you can sell the gown. The silver you earn for it will easily pay your way back to Venice, so long as you are prudent."

She bit her tongue as soon as she said it. Serafino and prudence were two words that could not coexist in the same sentence.

Nevertheless, Serafino appeared to reflect. "It was, indeed, a very fine gown." Then, to her relief, he smiled. "Very well, *cara*. I am staying at the inn with a *gufo* on its board. How do they say it here? An owl. See that I receive the gown by nightfall, along with its ruby studded girdle and those red slippers you also embroidered in gold, and all will be well."

He kissed her hand, then strolled away whistling a carefree tune.

He no sooner turned the corner out of her sight than she cursed herself for a fool. She had confessed to having brought one rich gown with her from Venice. As he had just shown, he clearly guessed that she had brought more: the jewelry, the perfume, the trinkets that she had gained in the house of Siri's first husband. He would never return to Venice where he had no one to blackmail to sustain his dissolute vices. Little by little he would bleed her dry here in Poitou, and when she had no more to give him, he would bleed dry her husband.

Her husband. Sir Balduin. Oh saints, oh saints! Only a quick, shaking palm to her lips smothered her gasp of despair. She could not let them meet. If Serafino knew she was to marry Sir Balduin— She must think of a way to stop Serafino before he betrayed the truth of her past and turned Sir Balduin's tender feelings for her to ugly, rancorous ashes as Serafino had done with her first love nearly thirty years ago.

She heard a familiar dragging footstep around the front of the shop.

"Did you see which way she went?" Sir Balduin queried someone. "Where do they sell pins for ladies' hair?"

Lucianna felt tears flowing over her fingers. She rubbed her face vigorously to scrub them away and to restore some color to a face that still felt too cold, then hurried around the side of shop to meet him.

"I am here," she said. "The silversmith did not have such a pin, but he promised to make one and send it to Siri."

"And I have the cloth," Sir Balduin said, hefting the package he carried for her view and adding with a smile, "paid for at a fair compromise, so there is nothing left to linger for. Unless you are hungry. There is an inn here that sells tolerable meals."

"*No.*" She realized she spoke too sharply, but if they should encounter Serafino at the inn— "The days are short in the fall. I do not like to ride the roads after dark, no matter how safe you say they are." Then she hesitated, even though Sir Balduin had already given a nod of assent to her reply. "Unless you are hungry and tired?" she queried. Sometimes riding followed by long hours of standing would make his wounded hip ache. Concern for him battled her worry about Serfino. "I saw a baker's shop as we rode into town. I am sure we could find something there to eat."

"To be truthful," Sir Balduin said, "I should be quite content sharing a snug supper at Vere, just the two of us." He slipped an arm around her waist, strong with a possessive tenderness, and began leading her towards the horses. "After all, we have a deal to talk about, you and I. Lady Siri is not the only one with plans to make for the future."

She felt some relief as he walked beside her with no sign of fatigue. He gave her a roguish smile—one from her best observations that he only shared with her—but she had not the heart to return it. How would she shield the joy he had brought her from Serafino? If she did not find a way, Sir Balduin's love would die beneath Serafino's meddling, whether at a slow wither or with one horrible, shattering blast. No, she could not—*would* not let that happen again.

Two

The wedding is off, *carissima!*" Lucianna held her head high as she swept across the sunlit chamber to where her former charge, Siri de Brielle, sat painting an elegant prayer book.

Siri shifted her swollen body. The child she carried made her increasingly uncomfortable as the days drew closer to the birth. Lucianna repressed a stir of guilt for adding to her distress, but she did not withdraw her pronouncement.

Siri's jewel blue eyes radiated dismay. "What, again? What happened this time?"

Lucianna had made her decision two weeks ago. She had but to maintain her resolve to put it into action. She had faltered twice already; she was determined not to waver again. If everyone at Vere Castle thought her irrational and unreasonable, all the better. This time she would cling to her fabricated offense no matter how tenaciously Sir Balduin cajoled her.

"He called me *paffuto*. I will have you know that my gowns fit me just as neatly as they did thirty years ago."

"Oh!" Siri said. "Oh, dear."

Trained in the art of illumination, Siri had insisted on ornamenting the little book of invocations and devotions with the very finest miniature paintings as a gift for Lucianna's wedding day. She worked on the book every morn. A cup of watered wine and a plate piled high with gingerbread sat on a table to the side of the slanted scribe's desk so that Siri could refresh herself while she worked. Lucianna set the food and drink aside, picked up the tray and buffed the metal surface with the wide green sleeve of her surcote, then examined her blurred reflection. She could make out little of her features, but her figure, which had always been curvaceous, remained neat and trim, despite passing her forty-fourth year last month.

"Perhaps you should stop trying to teach Sir Balduin Italian," Siri said. "I am sure he did not mean to call you plump."

"If he loved me as he says, he would pay stricter attention to my lessons. I have shown him the courtesy of learning his tongue. One would think it a small enough request that he should learn mine."

To an unfamiliar eye, the frown that pulled at Siri's full rosy lips would have appeared a pout, but Lucianna had known her since she was a babe and discerned the reproof Siri directed at her.

"Lucianna, you learned French with my mother in a nunnery in Venice before she married my father. Our minds are nimble when we are young. Sir Balduin—"

Lucianna cut off Siri's defense of the grey-haired knight. "Oh, *si*, he says he is too old to learn new things. 'Tis merely an excuse that will haunt our marriage. If he is too old to learn the difference between *paffuto* and *pazienza*, then he is too old to learn how to please a wife."

Siri's pout dissolved into sudden merriment, setting aglow the golden face that had bewitched their neighbors far and near and held her husband, Triston, joyfully smitten.

"Then perhaps," Siri said, "Sir Balduin forgot the word because you are not in the least *pazienza*. You know you are not, Lucianna, you are not patient at all!"

Lucianna gave a haughty sniff and put the tray back down. "How can one be patient in such a land as this? When men are not kissing you or trying to abscond with you behind my back, they are provoking quarrels with one another or reciting nonsensical poetry. The entire land is filled with *pazzi*."

"They are not madmen," Siri said with a tiny smile on her lips. She dipped a tapered brush into a vial of vermillion paint and resumed filling in the flowing scarlet dress of Mary Magdalene, clearly dismissing the seriousness of Lucianna's indignation. "And I do not know why you were so cross with Acelet's verses when he came for Christmas. We had poets in Venice, too. Some of them turned your eyes quite dreamy."

Lucianna moved to the window that overlooked the inner bailey of Vere Castle. Sir Balduin stood below, conversing with Siri's husband, Triston de Brielle. *Lord* Triston they called him now, since he had inherited the barony that had come to Siri through her late father. Sir Balduin was not as tall as his towering young master and his hair may have turned the color of slate, but the sight of him made Lucianna ache longingly for him. She had told herself a dozen times o'er the last two weeks that leaving was for the best, that she was too old to think of love. But she could not stop her sweet memories of him and how the rough-tongued soldier, Triston's most trusted advisor, had won over a heart she admitted was sometimes uncomfortably proud for those around her.

She caressed the emerald ring that graced her finger. Despite a number of gently amorous but chaste trysts, she had resisted all talk of marriage for over a year. She was too old, too settled in her ways to become a wife, she'd insisted. But last month, as her second summer closed in Poitou, Sir Balduin had made such a passionate plea of love that she had tossed aside her final doubts and let him slip his ring onto her hand. How she wished now that she had clung to her protective pride instead of allowing Sir Balduin's admiring glances, entreating smiles, and beguiling kisses to set her head spinning.

Serafino had not yet shown his face at Vere, but she knew it was only a matter of time. Lucianna could not endure a repeat of events in Venice. Unable, despite long sleepless, desperate nights to think of any other way to stop it, she had at last steeled her heart for the only answer. She must return to Venice and take Serafino with her.

But first she had to break off the wedding that now lay little more than a week away.

She took a quick step to the side of the window frame as she saw Sir Balduin turn his head and glance up in her direction. It would not have been the first time he caught her gazing down on him from Siri's workshop. If he cast another of his earnest, apologetic looks at her, Lucianna would not be able to cling to her determination.

She turned away from the window. "Your memories are flawed, *carissima*. I have not been dreamy for thirty years."

She fixed a brooding study on the tapestry on the opposite wall, a graceful boating scene. Though the construction of the vessels was different from the gondolas that had ferried her from place to place for the greater part of her life, the waves of the sea and swooping seagulls combined to stir nostalgic memories in her breast. She guessed a similar sentiment had prompted Siri to request its placement in her workshop.

"What happened thirty years ago?"

Siri's bright voice startled her. Lucianna bit briefly down on her lower lip. She had not meant to be so careless with her words.

"Nothing happened," she said. "I was a silly girl with romantic notions in my head, such as all young girls have, that is all."

Siri set down her paintbrush and swiveled about in her high backed scribe's chair to gaze at Lucianna. "You never tell me about your girlhood. Why? I know story after story about you and my mother when you were in the convent together, but they are all about *her*. I know my mother loved and trusted you, that she asked you to care for me before she died, that you have been as a second mother to me, but—"

"You know all you need to," Lucianna said.

33

She saw how Siri had reached around to rub the small of her back. Lucianna had never borne a child, but she recalled the backaches Siri's mother had complained of when she had carried Siri and her brother. Lucianna moved to stand behind the younger woman and gently knead her shoulders, neck and back. Siri had become distressed when it had taken her so many months to conceive after her marriage, but those days of worry were now past. She would give birth to a fine autumn baby. Lucianna's happiness for her mingled with grief that she would not be at Vere to see it.

Siri gave a long, low sigh at Lucianna's ministrations, but asked, "Why won't you tell me more?"

Lucianna repeated the same tale she always did. "Your mother and I met in the *convento di Santa Caterina* where her father sent her to be educated. We became the best of friends, but she was the daughter of a wealthy merchant, and I was not. She had a dowry to wed your father, I had not a *denaro* to my name. I am now as I was then, a spinster who did not wish to be a nun, so your mother took me into her home with her when she became a wife."

"But—"

"Do not be tedious, *carissima*. There is nothing of interest to tell. I am content as I am. Or I will be once I return to Venice."

She waited for Siri's protest, prepared to counter every plea and argument as she had twice before. It was not entirely unsatisfying that Siri, a new young wife herself, still longed for Lucianna's companionship. But returning was the only solution Lucianna could see, though she could never admit the reason to Siri.

But this time, when Siri caught Lucianna's hands and pulled her around so that she could gaze at her, Siri's face was crumpled with laughter rather than entreaty. "Lucianna, do not be absurd. Because Sir Balduin misspoke a word of Italian? That is your silliest reason for calling off the wedding yet!"

"I could not agree more."

Lucianna did her best to quench the tremor that wove through her at the sound of Sir Balduin's voice. He must indeed have glimpsed her from the window and came now to confront her. Like Siri, he had called their argument absurd, but Lucianna had no other choice. She loved him too much marry him.

"Is it silly," she demanded, "to wish to be admired by my husband, rather than likened to a *maiale*?"

Siri's gasp raked across the puzzlement on Sir Balduin's face. "Lucianna! I do not believe Sir Balduin called you a pig, even by mistake!"

Lucianna tried to take advantage of Sir Balduin's horror to sweep past him while he was too stunned to stop her, but she heard the uneven tread of his footsteps as he followed her through the doorway. She quickened her pace, but he caught her at the head of the stairs and pulled her around to face him.

"Lucianna, I know my tongue is clumsy — too clumsy to please you by learning the language of your birth. But in French I call you truly sweetheart, dear one, beloved, angel! Our wedding is a week from Friday. Do not let us quarrel again."

She almost let him draw her into his arms. No one had ever called her angel! But when she reached out a hand to set it to his waist, it fell upon the leather pouch that jingled with silver at his belt. She wiggled away before he could kiss her.

"*No.* I have given you three chances and you have failed them all. I will not marry a man who refuses to trust me with his thoughts —"

"That is not true," Sir Balduin protested. "What cause have I given you to think I do not trust you?"

"Last week when you sat with me in the gardens while I embroidered the baptismal gown, I asked you what you were thinking and you said you were thinking of nothing. You would not share the truth with me no matter how I begged you, and when I persisted you grew annoyed with me."

"Exasperated, not annoyed," he said, "because I was not

thinking of anything except how the sun was making me sleepy. I told you that, but you went all cross and said it was impossible to have a mind so empty and that you could not marry a man who would not confide in you, and the next thing I knew you said the wedding was off." A small, mischievous smile that he had not shared with her until weeks into their courting played now across his lips. "But then I leaned over and nuzzled your ear and you changed your mind."

He bent forward, clearly aiming again for that same vulnerable spot, but she ignored the eager thump in her breast and took a vigorous step out of reach.

"*Si*, I forgave you, and how did you repay me? With base inconsideration."

Sir Balduin sighed. His toe began to beat one of its rare, impatient patterns. "Lucianna, I have apologized a dozen times for missing dinner. If I had known that Lord Laurant would be out hunting when Triston sent me to speak with him, I would have waited to leave Vere until after we dined."

"You might have sent a servant to tell me you would be late."

"I did not think it important."

Lucianna's always precise posture snapped even more rigid.

Sir Balduin's toe ceased its tapping. Apparently recognizing that he had offended yet again, said quickly, "Forgive me, my love, it was thoughtless and selfish of me, as you say. But in fairness, how was I to know you had asked the kitchens to prepare my favorite dish?"

"It was to be a surprise. Oh!" She flung up her hands. "You are hopeless! You refuse to confide in me, you have no respect for my feelings, and now you call me fat! I will endure no more of this."

She turned towards the stairs.

"Lucianna—"

She twitched her arm away from his reaching clasp. "*No.*

As soon as I arrange for an escort, I am going back to Venice. And that is *finale.*"

She ran down the stairs, ignoring his calling voice, pausing only when she knew herself safely out of his sight in the middle of the hall to stop and dry her tears with her sleeve. She had severed their engagement twice before, only to crumble before his apologies and coaxings and ear nuzzlings and murmured endearments. She must not give him the chance to persuade her to yield again. She knew if she lingered too long he would follow her, so she turned her steps to the castle's exit.

Her fingers found and stroked the great stone of his ring. She ought to return it to him, but she had no money of her own to hire escorts and she dared not ask Siri to lend her a guard, lest Siri and Sir Balduin between them convince her to change her mind. She could not sell it, not after she had guarded it so zealously from Serafino. But she could pretend, and had made arrangements to do just that. While Sir Balduin had been off on an errand for Triston, she had taken a groom as escort and returned to the market town. There she had found a goldsmith who had agreed to lend her money in exchange for the ring, and then to hold the jewel until Sir Balduin repaid him the sum she had "borrowed." The silver from the goldsmith would pay her way back to Venice. She had already left a note in her chamber telling Sir Balduin where to retrieve his ring. He would be horrified when he learned she had sold the gift of his love, but in truth, that would be for the best. Let him think her obstinate, irrational, ungrateful and mercenary. Anything but learn the truth.

Lucianna sniffled dolefully, her eyes so full of a fresh swell of tears that she did not recognize the man standing in the bailey with Triston until Triston's shout checked her path to the stables.

"Lady Lucianna! You have a visitor, come all the way from Venice."

Lucianna's hand clenched against her stomach. *Oh, no, no,*

no, no! She turned, hurriedly blinking dry her eyes as Triston crossed the courtyard to join her. At his side strode a man with a face like an angel, haloed with thick auburn hair a few shades darker than her own but silvered like hers at the temples.

"Cara!" Serafino swept her into his arms, briefly smothering her against the fine, fresh linen of a bright blue surcote he had undoubtedly sold her gown to purchase. *"Mia sorella! Don* Triston tells me you are about to marry. I have come just in time."

Three

Sir Balduin limped across the bailey, frowning at the handsome, auburn-haired man boldly embracing the woman he loved.

"Lucianna?" he queried as he came abreast of them standing with Triston.

The stranger turned, his arm still draped around Lucianna's waist, but it was Triston who answered with a reassuring clap to Sir Balduin's shoulder. "It is only her brother, old friend."

Sir Balduin felt his cheeks warm. Had his jealousy been so obvious? But he shot a surprised look at Lucianna.

"Brother?" She had never mentioned any kin to him before.

The auburn-haired man released her and gave Sir Balduin a bow as graceful as his elegant figure and beatifically handsome face. "I am Serafino Fabio, at your service, *signore*. And you?" He spoke French with the same accent as Lucianna, somewhat thicker but not indecipherably so.

Triston laughed. "This is the bridegroom, Sir Balduin de Soler."

"But no!" Lucianna exclaimed. "We are not to marry. It is over! Serafino, you must take me back to Venice. Now!"

Sir Balduin's heart gave a panicked lurch. Though her previous threats had alarmed him, as Triston always pointed out, unless Siri agreed to her demands Lucianna had no resources to pay for her return to Venice. And since Siri invariably dallied over pleasing Lucianna on this point, Sir Balduin always had the time to find a way to soothe whatever feathers he had inadvertently ruffled on this lovely, temperamental woman. But a brother to escort her safely along the highways back to the lands she still called home?

"Lucianna, please, I beg you—" Sir Balduin had never pled for mercy from any man, not even the one who had shattered his hip with a sword blow and then stood with steel aimed over his heart before Triston had cut the villain down. But it seemed since Lucianna had crossed the threshold of Vere Castle he had done little else than beg her pardon, and never more frequently than over the last fortnight as their wedding at last drew near. He had spoken the words so many times now, they no longer felt awkward on his tongue, but they fell more urgently than they ever had before. "Just let me speak to you alone."

"There is nothing left to say. Serafino, come!"

Even Triston looked dismayed when she took Serafino's arm and sought to drag him off to the stables.

But Serafino withstood her with a laugh Sir Balduin suspected had charmed many a woman. "What, *cara*, would you break this gentleman's heart? Look at the way he gazes on you."

Sir Balduin prayed she would do just that and read the heart she would, indeed, break if she left. But Lucianna only stuck her nose in the air and looked pointedly over Sir Balduin's shoulder.

"He adores you, *cara*," Serafino said with the insight Lucianna continued to snub. "*No, no*, I cannot allow you to walk away from love again."

Again?

Serafino pried something from Lucianna's clenched fist— Sir Balduin's ring!—and slid it back onto her finger.

Serafino flashed a smile as beautiful as an angel at Sir Balduin. "She is a stubborn, volatile woman, *signore*, but you will never be bored with her. *Don* Triston says I arrived in time for a wedding, and a wedding we will have."

"You will, of course, be our guest," Triston said. "Lucianna, take your brother inside. See that he is refreshed from his journey and have the servants prepare my brother's room for his stay." Triston glanced at the bay horse with the white blaze down its nose that Serafino had left near the stable. A single saddlebag draped the mount's hindquarters. "Surely you traveled with more than this?"

"My packhorse lost a shoe a few villages down the road, but with my destination nigh, I did not wish to tarry so much as an hour to embrace my sister again. I left orders for my things to be sent after me."

Sir Balduin saw a fresh pucker appear between Lucianna's gracefully arched brows, but almost immediately his gaze dipped to his ring again. Why had she been holding rather than wearing it? The other times they had quarreled, she had left it on her finger until he had coaxed himself back into her favor. Had he truly overstepped some irreparable bound by mispronouncing the Italian she insisted on trying to teach him? He was quite certain he had not called her fat. *Grassa* was too near the French *grasse* for him to have made that mistake. There were other words he could not make heads or tails of, though. Her brother was right, her temperament was volatile, to say the least, but that was what made Sir Balduin feel so alive when he was with her.

Serafino thanked Triston in his engaging way, then nudged Lucianna towards the keep. Sir Balduin held his breath, fearful of her refusal to stay. After a moment of clear hesitance, she gave one of the sniffs that betrayed her vexation, but led her brother inside.

Sir Balduin's gaze lingered on her retreating form until she vanished within the walls of the keep. Then he felt the clasp of Triston's hand on his shoulder.

"Do not take this question amiss," Triston said, "but the Lady Lucianna is a—" he paused, appearing to weigh his words, finally settling on "—complicated woman. Are you sure you will be happy with her?"

Sir Balduin studied his master with his formidable height, impressive shoulders, wildly handsome looks, and most of all, his youth.

"I served your father for over thirty years," Sir Balduin said, "as a knight of his household. He housed me, fed me, paid me enough to clothe myself and enjoy a roll of the dice now and then, but not enough to support a wife. I was content with that, or thought I was. Then four years ago, you succeeded your father."

An autumn breeze ruffled the hair at the nape of his neck. He smoothed the rippled fringe back down, recalling as he too frequently did since Lucianna's arrival, how swiftly his hair had greyed and coarsened after the injury to his hip.

"You placed your trust in me by listening to my counsel," he continued, "set me to train your men-at-arms, and asked me to ride chief at your side when you rode into battle. And you paid me so generously that for the first time in my life, I had money beyond my immediate needs. I thought myself too old by then to think of marriage, but then Lucianna came with Lady Siri and after a time, she smiled on me, and sir—" He paused. He did not think a man of twenty-eight could understand, but he said it anyway. "She made me feel young again. Now you have offered to make me castellan of one of Lady Siri's new castles, and there is no woman I would rather have by my side than the Lady Lucianna while I serve you there."

Triston nodded, more supportively, Sir Balduin feared, than approvingly. A misunderstanding on the day Lady Siri had arrived at Vere Castle had cast Triston in Lucianna's fiery disfavor until he had redeemed himself by rescuing Siri from a villain who had sought to abduct her and force her into an unwanted marriage. Because Lucianna claimed to have forgiven all had not, however, turned her former suspicions into fawning benevolence of Triston, and Sir Balduin still sometimes caught Triston gazing at her a bit dubiously. Sir Balduin suspected Triston would be relieved to have him marry her and carry her off to Siri's castle.

42

"But she has broken off the wedding for the third time," Sir Balduin added, with a sigh. "Sir, you have a wife. How do you manage to please her?"

Triston had borne a stormy temper from his youth, but since his marriage to Siri the demons that had driven him had appeared to find some peace. He looked thoughtful for a moment, then said, "Well, Siri likes it when I pluck her flowers from the garden and tie them into a cluster with ribbons."

"I made up to Lucianna with flowers after I was late to dinner last week." Her kisses in the aftermath of that quarrel had been most satisfying. "But she was so very cross this time after I called her—well, I am not sure what I called her in Italian, though I am certain it was not what she says I said. But she is enraged with me anyway, and this time she took off my ring. Her brother made her put it back on, but I fear it will take more than blossoms to keep it there."

Triston began strolling towards the stable, presumably to give orders for the care of Serafino's horse. "As I said, she is a difficult—er, complicated woman."

He slid a quick glance at Sir Balduin's face as Sir Balduin fell into step beside him, apparently worried he'd offended, but Sir Balduin brushed it aside with a small sweep of his hand. Love had not blinded him to his beloved's flaws, but he possessed enough of his own to refrain from judging her too harshly. Patience, fortunately, was one quality he'd learned to cultivate early in his life, for it had served him well through the years, keeping him from the sort of useless, hot blooded quarrels that had hindered the advancement of many of his peers. He suspected his even temperament had been one of the traits that had prompted Triston to seek his counsel after his father's death, as a balance for his own impulsive, hotheaded nature.

Sir Balduin had been startled to find his patience occasionally strained when Lucianna insisted on drilling him on those baffling Italian words that veered so differently from the sound and form of his French. But save for those infrequent instances, he trusted that his quiet disposition would be equally effective in his marriage with Lucianna as it had in his service to the house de Brielle.

But he would never know if she returned to Venice. Dread again shivered through him at the thought, stirring up the tenacious persistence that too many men had underestimated because he chose to control both his temper and his tongue.

"I cannot allow her to leave me over a silly misunderstanding," he said with a determined force. "I must think of something —"

Triston stopped and spun suddenly on his heel to face him. "Paint!"

"Paint?" Had his young master gone addled?

"Siri's moods have been dismayingly erratic of late. It alarmed me at first, for you know how ordinarily she is the most cheerful woman in the world. Lady Lucianna says it is because of the babe and that Siri will cease to snap at me once the child is born."

Triston's expression suggested sincere hope that Lucianna's promise might be fulfilled, and quickly.

He continued, "When I told Siri that I did not care what her grandfather's name was, I refused to consider Cosimo as a name should she bear a boy, she became so cross she refused to speak to me for days. After three days of chilled silence between us, the idea came to me. I went to Normandy, to the scriptorium where her father learned to illuminate, and consulted with the monks. For a generous donation, they gave me a brilliant red paint called vermillion which they told me was almost as expensive as gold. I believe Siri is using some of it in the prayer book she's illuminating for Lucianna's wedding gift. Siri has been nothing but smiles and laughter since."

"And your son's name?" Sir Balduin asked curiously.

Triston grinned. "She agreed she could be quite content with Simon."

The name of Siri's late brother. Triston had already bestowed his own paternal grandfather's name on the son of his first marriage, Pierre, though they all called the lad Perrin.

Sir Balduin smiled slowly. "I see. I do not think paint is my answer, but I take your point and believe I know something that may gratify Lucianna nearly as well. May I have your leave to visit Poitiers, sir? I should not be gone above a week." Indeed, he fully intended to return in time to win back her consent for their wedding day to go forward.

"Certainly," Triston said. "Take whatever time you need. I will second Siri in stalling any more threats of Lucianna's to fly to Venice while you're gone. From the look of him, I suspect we will have her brother's help in that. He questioned me earnestly about his sister's happiness before you joined us. He appears most fond of her and seemed sincerely elated when I told him she was soon to marry my most trusted knight and advisor."

Sir Balduin smiled at the praise. After his initial, jealous survey of the man, his attention had been too focused on Lucianna to scrutinize her brother closely, so he accepted Triston's judgment.

"I will see her brother's horse cared for first, and then —"

"Nay, I will do that," Triston said. "Return to the keep and begin what preparations you need for your journey."

Sir Balduin thanked him, then limped back to the keep to count out the silver Triston had paid him that morning, jingling in the pouch tied to his belt.

11

Convento di Santa Caterina ~ Venice 1148

*W*ould you not rather help me read this?" Elisabetta asked. "Or trace our letters or add our sums, or by Saint Catherine, even practice our French? How can you bear to sit all day and stitch and stitch and stitch?"

Elisabetta always referred to her lessons from Sister Maria Angela in the plural, even though Lucianna was never allowed to read or write or add or even speak while the nun instructed their "guest." But after reverting to her tearful wailing twice when Sister Maria Angela had tried to dismiss Luicianna to the herb garden several weeks into Elisabetta's lessons, the nun had capitulated once and for all to Lucianna's permanent place next to Elisabetta in the chapel attached to the almonry. When Sister Maria Angela's back was turned, Lucianna caught Elisabetta's triumphant smile. A year had passed and she no longer wept for her home, Elisabetta whispered between their beds at night, but only at the thought of losing Lucianna's companionship.

"I have learned to read better than you by watching over your shoulder," Lucianna said. She had had no interest in any of the subjects at first, but she had not been able to avoid absorbing the knowledge as she watched and listened, until at last she had begun to enjoy the lessons, too. She dipped her bone needle again into the cloth. She hated the way the threads dragged through the linen. Why would they not let her use the bronze needles yet? Her ten-year-old *hands had grown ever so much from a year ago!* "I can speak French as well as you, too."

That they also whispered to one another in the dark while Sister Maria Angela snored loudly from her bed down the row near the doorway.

Elisabetta set aside the book she had been reading aloud and took up her wax tablet and stylus. "You cannot learn to write by merely watching," she said and began to draw in the wax.

"Nor you how to improve your embroidery," Lucianna retorted. Her voice was prim as she stabbed her needle through the cloth again. She and Elisabetta had grown to tease and laugh about a great many things, but Lucianna never jested about something as important as stitchery.

Elisabetta lay in a dreadfully inelegant posture in the grass, flat on her stomach with her skirts spread all helter-skelter about her ankles while she propped herself up on her elbows to draw her letters. Sister Maria Angela frowned whenever she saw such disgraceful behavior and tried to rebuke the girl, but since she never switched her, Elisabetta had learned to ignore the scoldings. Lucianna might have paced restlessly if she had not had her embroidery to keep her still, but she did not think she could ever be daring enough to sprawl in the grass. She straightened her back a little instead and pushed through another stitch.

"Is your father coming for Christmas again?" Lucianna asked while she outlined a small shield. Sister Maria Angela said that linens with decorative shields were popular among knights willing to part with some silver, especially if the shields contained the device of their house. Lucianna was certain she could stitch a crenelated tower inside of this one if she only had a better needle.

Elisabetta nodded. The red highlights in her dark hair shown fiery in the summer sun. Lucianna's auburn locks seemed always the same to her eye, whether she sat indoors or out.

"He sent me a letter again, just to see if I could read it," Elisabetta said. "He says he will come every Christmas and Easter to see me, so I must study very hard and show him what I have learned. He wants me to write him a reply." She glanced up at Lucianna.

"You are sure the nuns know nothing of your parents?"

She had asked it many times o'er the last year. Lucianna always answered the same. "If they do, they have told me nothing."

"Then how do you know your father's name was Panfilo?"

Lucianna shrugged and closed the outline of the shield.

"Why will you not tell me? I have kept no secrets from you."

"It is not a secret," Lucianna said quickly, stung by the hurt in Elisabetta's voice. "It is only — special. I do not want it mocked."

Elisabetta sat up, her dark eyes a-flash. "You think I would mock you?"

"Speak softer," Lucianna hissed. She regretted that her words had aggrieved her friend. She had grown to trust Elisabetta as she trusted her own heart. But — "It is not you I fear, it is Sister Maria Angela. If she came upon us and heard me, she would laugh, or perhaps she would scold and say I made it up and then she might call me devil child. That is what she did when she made me pick berries for the infirmary from the barberry bush and I called it an evil plant for pricking my fingers so badly that I could not stitch for a week."

Elisabetta eyes widened in awe. "Is that not the one known as the Holy Thorn?"

Lucianna nodded with a sigh. "Because it was part of the crown of thorns borne by Our Lord upon the cross. But I was not thinking of that when it pricked me. Sister Maria Angela said I had spoken a blasphemy — "

" — and switched you," Elisabetta finished before Lucianna could. Lucianna nodded again. Elisabetta pressed her lips together very tightly.

"I do not want her to say that my father's name is wicked, too," Lucianna said. "And so I must keep how I know to myself forever and ever."

But this Elisabetta would not agree to. "You shall not keep it from me. You will whisper it to me tonight between our beds while Sister Maria Angela snores so loudly that she will not be able to hear us."

Lucianna hesitated, but Elisabetta appeared to feel the matter settled, for she cast a mischievous glance at the cloth in Lucianna's *hands and changed the subject. "My father will want me to tell him about my embroidery, too, when I write."*

"You mean how you pull the threads too tightly and bunch the cloth?" Lucianna gave a sniff of impatience. How could anyone find it so difficult to embroider, even with a bone needle?

"Then I must practice before winter comes," Elisabetta said merrily. "So we must trade places. Let me finish your pattern and you shall finish my sentence." She motioned at her tablet.

Lucianna frowned at her. "I will not sit in the grass."

"And I do not want to sit on that stuffy old bench, but I suppose I must learn to sit up straight someday if I am to marry a lord."

"Then come sit beside me. I will let you stitch on this corner." Lucianna indicated the lower, empty bottom of the cloth. Much as she loved Elisabetta, she did not want the other girl to ruin her shield.

Elisabetta stood up and shook out her skirts, though no amount of brushing with her hand would wipe away the grass stains. Her father must be very rich, Lucianna thought, not to mind how many gowns his careless daughter ruined. She handed her cloth and needle to Elisabetta in trade for the tablet and stylus, then exchanged a smile with the other girl as Elisabetta sat on the bench. Her friend had written Elisabetta e Luci *in the wax.*

Lucianna watched with a critical eye as Elisabetta begin to embroider, offering helpful hints for how to keep the stitches straight and the cloth smooth. Only when Elisabetta appeared to have found a rhythm did Lucianna press the stylus into the wax and finish the thought Elisabetta had written so many times before.

Elisabetta e Lucianna, sorelle sempre.

Elisabetta leaned her head on Lucianna's shoulder — Lucianna had grown tall quicker than she — and murmured while she continued to stitch, "Always sisters."

Lucianna rubbed out the words before Sister Maria Angela could see them, but whispered back, "Always sisters."

In the dark of the night, Lucianna hoped Elisabetta had forgotten their conversation outside the dormitory window, but when Sister Maria Angela began to snore, Elisabetta's hand sought and found Lucianna's. They often fell asleep with hands clasped between their beds.

"Now you will tell me about your father," Elisabetta murmured, using the French they always practiced in the veiling shadows.

The faint mist of moonlight that slipped through the window allowed Lucianna to make out the shape of the broad, thick beams of the ceiling overhead. Elisabetta spoke with such certainty that Lucianna knew it would be an insult to their friendship to refuse her.

"He came to me in a dream." She paused, retracing every image, every emotion she had experienced that night. It took her a few moments to find confidence in the foreign words she needed, but when they came, they did so in a flow. "It was just before you came to the convent, perhaps by a month. My body was very sore, for Sister Maria Angela had made me scrub and scrub and scrub in the kitchen all day. I remember crying because I ached so badly – " softly, of course, so that the nun should not hear " – but at last I fell asleep, very deeply. And then he came to me, a man in a golden light. I could not see his face because the light was so bright, but I did not feel afraid. He said, 'I belong to you.' That startled me, for I sensed I did not know him. I asked him his name and he said, 'Panfilo.' And as he said it, I felt – " again she paused, until Elisabetta's fingers pressed on hers. "I felt loved. And I felt safe. And then he was gone." She shrugged her shoulders against the bolster that propped her up. "He did not say he was my father, but who else could he have been?"

"Panfilo," Elisabetta murmured against the background of Sister Maria Angela's snores. "Did your mother come to you, as well?"

"No, only he. And just that once."

"But you call her Rosaria, because the name is pretty. I think it is pretty, too."

Lucianna did not realize she had been holding her body tensely until she heard the smile in Elisabetta's voice. She had not truly thought her friend would mock or laugh at her, but now that she had shared the dream, a sweet relaxation seeped into her. She slid her fingers so that they laced with Elisabetta's.

Now we will drift to sleep.

"Lucianna."

"Hmmm?"

"The nuns know nothing of your parents and your dream told you nothing but a name. If you could choose who they were, who would they be?"

The question made Lucianna vaguely testy. "I have never thought of it. Let me go to sleep."

"You must have thought of it," Elisabetta insisted. "If it were me, I would think about it every day." Lucianna shifted uncomfortably in the bed. It must have made her fingers twitch, for Elisabetta exclaimed, though softly, "See? I did not laugh at your dream. Tell me how you imagine them to be."

Lucianna knew Elisabetta would not let the question alone until she either answered or Sister Maria Angela snorted herself awake.

"I know it is wicked and vain," she at last confessed, "but I wish they had been rich, so that I could wear gowns as soft as yours. The ones they make me wear here always itch."

Elisabetta had let her try on one of her silken gowns once. How they had giggled and giggled in their haste for Lucianna to draw it on, strut about the empty dormitory, and pull it off again before Sister Maria Angela came upon them.

"Let us say they were wealthy merchants, like my father is," Elisabetta whispered. "Which one of them had hair your color?"

Lucianna considered, then said, "My mother, of course. A woman named Rosaria should have reddish hair, don't you think?"

There was a small silence into which she thought perhaps Elisabetta yawned.

"I love your hair," Elisabetta murmured when she spoke again. "It is the color of leaves in autumn. What other name did they go by?"

"You mean like Gallo?" Elisabetta's surname. "I do not know. I cannot even guess at that."

"We shall make something up. We shall begin tomorrow to weave together the most splendid family for you."

Another silence. Another yawn? Although she could not see it, Lucianna yawned, too. "I wish their name was Gallo, like yours. I wish we were truly sisters."

"It cannot be Gallo." *Elisabetta sounded as sad as Lucianna felt.* "But that does not matter. Remember what I wrote in the wax."

What we *wrote in the wax, Lucianna thought as her lids grew heavy.* Elisabetta and Lucianna, always sisters.

Elisabetta squeezed her hand three times, her signal that she was finally ready to sleep. Lucianna squeezed back twice, and slid into the slumber that had become so peaceful since her heart had entwined with the girl's in the bed next to hers.

Four

Lucianna gazed down at the three silver needles bedded against the red silk lining of the tiny but beautifully carved casket that held them, and nearly burst into tears. In the house of Siri's first husband, a wealthy Venetian merchant, she had usually embroidered with needles of iron or bronze. These must have been shockingly expensive. Even with his prominent position in Triston's household, the pins must have cost months of Sir Balduin's pay. He still looked a little pale as he waited for her response, as though he had not quite recovered from the massive loss of his coins, but he also looked touchingly hopeful that they would please her.

Please her? No man had ever given her a finer gift. These would make her threads slide through cloth like butter.

Her lips trembled to thank him in the sweetest way for a couple in love, with a kiss that forgave everything in the past and promised only bliss in their future. But even as her feet quivered to carry her into Sir Balduin's arms, Serafino spoke from where he gazed at the gift over her shoulder.

"There, you see, *cara*? You have been cross for no good reason. Today Sir Balduin lavishes silver needles on you. Tomorrow it will be gold threads for your embroidery and silk gowns for you to wear and black pepper at every meal, imported all the way from Venice."

Siri's first husband had dabbled in the import and sale of black pepper, known as "the king of spices" for its expense. Lucianna had developed a fond taste for it when she had companioned Siri in her first marriage and had often lamented its absence from Triston's table. But Lucianna shrank at her brother's words. They were only a reminder of the poison he would pour into her marriage if she allowed the needles to melt her heart, as she had the sweet posy of flowers Sir Balduin had brought her after she had rebuked him for missing dinner.

She snapped the pretty little casket shut. "All I see is a man who expects me to sew my fingers to the bone for him. Shirts, hats—no doubt he will even want embroidery on his shoes!" She shoved the casket back into Sir Balduin's hands. "*No*. I will not live my life as a drudge, just to wipe away the shame of never being a wife. Take him away, Serafino, out of my sight!"

She tried to slam the door of her bedchamber, but Serafino, who had stepped into the corridor outside to view the needles, stuck his foot on the threshold and blocked it from closing.

"*Signore*," he said with a reassuring smile at Sir Balduin, "you must not heed her. I'm afraid I carelessly reminded her this morning that she is no spring maid as I sought to laud her good fortune in winning the favor of so generous a knight as yourself, but she took my remarks quite amiss. See, Lucianna, how I was right to praise him, though. You will lack for no luxury as his wife, while all he asks in return is to show off a bit of your fine embroidery to his friends. Be reasonable, *cara*."

Lucianna determined to be anything but. If nagging and scolding and peevish rebukes had failed to break Sir Balduin's affection for her, then she must leave him in no doubt that his "insulting gift" had broken hers.

"I will not be a slave to his vanity, any more than I will tolerate his disrespect for my feelings or aspersions upon my appearance." She met Sir Balduin's earnest eyes, allowing the blaze of fury she felt for Serafino to fill her own. "Go. Leave me. Do not ask to see me again. I am returning to Venice, where I shall wipe the dust of this vile land and all who live here from my shoes."

Sir Balduin opened his mouth to protest. She did not dare let him speak, not when she already felt her throat thickening with tears. She jerked off his emerald ring and hurled it at his chest.

"Take it and go!"

As Sir Balduin fumbled to catch the unexpected missile, Lucianna lifted one of her still Poitevin-dusted shoes and stomped it on Serafino's foot. Serafino flinched and howled, allowing Lucianna to kick his foot away from the threshold and slam her chamber door.

She flung herself on her bed and wept as she had not wept for nearly thirty years. She should have known better than to open her heart to love again, not after Serafino had ruined everything when she had been fifteen. She had not even known she had a brother until he had shown up on the doorstep of Elisabetta's father's house. Even then, she and Elisabetta had managed, with Serafino's cooperation, to conceal their relationship from everyone, except the one person who had mattered most to Lucianna . . . Vincenzo Mirolli. Elisabetta had died with the secret still unspoken. Even Elisabetta's daughter, Siri, had not known until Serafino had come riding into the yard at Vere Castle that Lucianna possessed a living relative in the world.

Now Serafino had returned to ruin everything . . . again!

She wept so brokenly that she did not hear the soft knock on her door or the muted click of its opening and realize she was no longer alone until she felt a gentle hand stroking her back. The touch startled her into trying to choke off the sobs by pressing her face deeper into the blankets.

"Lucianna," Siri whispered, "what is the matter? I have never seen you like this before."

Oh, heavens. That Siri, whose tears Lucianna had dried at

her parents' death, whom she had comforted when he first husband died, and held weeping after the illness that took her brother, should now witness Lucianna sobbing like a child . . . Lucianna pushed herself up and scrubbed at the tears on her cheeks with a brisk, determined hand.

"'Tis nothing, *carissima*," she said, though her voice came out thick with the fresh tears welling there. "I am a foolish, foolish woman, is all. This Poitevin air is unhealthy for me. It is my great joy that you have found happiness here, but I—I must return to the tranquility I knew in Venice."

Though Siri's eyes remained serious and a little frightened, a mischievous smile very like her mother's flitted over her lips. "Lucianna, you were never tranquil. I know some have called you proud"—Siri's father—"—and meddling"—Siri's brother when Lucianna had let Siri marry Alessandro in his absence—"and imperious"—ah, that was Siri's new husband, Triston—"but you have never been anything but a tender second mother to me." Siri sat on the bed beside her. "*I* think you have only been discontent. And I have never asked you why." Siri slid her hand into Lucianna's and squeezed it.

She was so like Elisabetta, not in face, but in her loving, loyal heart and spirit. It shamed Lucianna to be caught thus in a mire of self-pity. The young should not have to comfort the old. She blinked away her lingering tears.

"It is the silliest thing, *carissima*. I am merely overcome with homesickness. I shall be quite content once I am in Venice again."

"With Serafino? Why did you never tell me you had a brother?"

Lucianna pulled her hand gently free of Siri's and rose from the bed. She crossed to the wardrobe cabinet where hung the many fine gowns Siri's first husband had bestowed on Lucianna to make his young wife happy. The sleek black gown that she had embellished with golden embroidery on the bodice was missing now, as so many others had vanished through the years to keep Serafino quiet. It had to stop, finally and forever. And that could only happen if Lucianna returned to Venice.

She could not tell Siri or anyone the truth, not all of it. But anger and frustration drove her to lash out with as much of the truth as she dared.

"Because he is and always has been an embarrassment to me." She snapped shut the wardrobe door and turned towards Siri. "He is a gambler and a spendthrift and revels in many other vices that it would shock your ears to hear and shame my tongue to speak. I have spent my life trying to avoid him." And failing miserably. "I left Venice hoping never to see him again, but now he has found me here. He will ruin the peace of all of us if I let him stay. But he will follow me back to Venice if I go, and leave the rest of you untroubled."

"Even if it means leaving Sir Balduin?" Siri asked.

"Love is for the young, *carissima*. It was foolish of me to forget that."

Siri smiled at her from the bed. Her golden beauty had come from her father, but that smile again was Elisabetta's. "I think one is never too old to love, and Sir Balduin adores you. You will break his heart if you leave us." She rose and crossed to take one of Lucianna's hands in hers. "Are you afraid he will judge you for your brother's sins? I am certain he loves you too much for that. But if Serafino's presence worries you so, I will have Triston speak with him. He can drop Serafino a very strong hint to behave himself while he's here."

Oh, heavens, a conversation like that and Triston might evict Lucianna from Vere, rather than letting her leave it of her own choice with her head still held high.

Lucianna drew her hand away before her fingers betrayed her agitation. "That is not necessary. Serafino is annoying, but I am not leaving because of him. I am going because this marriage would be a mistake. We may or may not be too old to love, but one thing is sure, we are each too old to change. *Signor* Balduin has too many faults I cannot tolerate and try as

57

I might, I cannot control my tongue. I will become a wretched nag. I will pick apart his love until he despises me instead, and that I could not bear." It was likely true. Perhaps it was well that Serafino had come. The dismal thought made her chest ache. "It is best this way, *carissima*, that I go while we each still bear fond memories of the other."

Siri's teeth chewed on her berry-ripe lower lip for a moment. Her brow puckered in such a manner that Lucianna began gathering together more arguments to counter whatever protests fell next from Siri's tongue.

"Would you grant me one favor before you go?"

The question startled Lucianna. She had expected more resistance to her words.

"Of course, *carissima*." Lucianna reached out and brushed Siri's golden locks with loving fingers.

"Then will you at least wait until after the baby is born?"

"Oh!" Lucianna gave a quick shake of her head. "That will be another month. I cannot possibly linger here that much longer."

Siri's blue eyes darkened with an expression her brave, bright spirit rarely revealed. Fear.

"Please, Lucianna? I am so excited and joyful for this babe" —her hand caressed her belly where the child grew— "but I—I am also a little afraid. It would be easier if my mother were here, but you have been as a second mother to me all my life. Lucianna, I need you with me for the birth. Please!"

Lucianna felt the tug of both affection and reluctance. She had never borne a child herself, but she had helped Siri's mother through the births of her two babes. But a month! So long for Serafino to cause more mischief! So long to hold Sir Balduin at bay while she ached day and night to spend her life with him.

"Please?" Siri said more softly. "I need you. And I want little Simon to meet you before you go." Her other hand joined the first to rest lovingly on her swollen belly.

Lucianna felt herself embraced with the babe in Siri's smile. She struggled to hold her resolve. "That is foolish, *carissima*. He will not remember me."

"He will know you as I do, for I shall tell him of you every day."

Lucianna felt her resistant core melting against all her better judgment. "What if it is not a boy?"

"Then I shall tell Elisabetta."

"Triston has agreed to name a daughter for your mother?"

"Well . . . that, or 'Alyne,' for his. I still have time to persuade him."

"And win yourself some more costly paints if you turn on him the pout you gave him when he rejected 'Cosimo.'"

Lucianna almost joined her laughter with Siri's over that memory, until she remembered Sir Balduin's own costly gift of the silver needles and felt her breast pang again. But she had loved and cared for Siri far too long to turn her back on the young woman's plea.

"Very well, *carissima*, but only if you promise me that you will respect my decision about Sir Balduin and not seek to make me change my mind."

From the way Siri bit her lip again, Lucianna knew she had hoped to make use of Lucianna's consent to do just that, but Lucianna held the blue gaze sternly until Siri finally nodded her head. Then it would be well. Siri had been the most enthusiastic supporter of Sir Balduin's courtship. Triston would be no trouble. Lucianna had frequently glimpsed doubt in his eyes at his most trusted retainer's object of affection. Triston would offer no encouragement to Sir Balduin to continue his pursuit if Lucianna continued to treat him with disdain. As for Serafino . . . so long as Lucianna held firm, there would be nothing he could do but follow her to Venice in failure once Siri's baby was born.

Five

Sir Balduin was sure Triston meant to be helpful by sending him back to Poitiers. He had not come to the capitol in search of a peacemaking gift for Lucianna this time, but rather with a commission to check on Triston's young cousin, Acelet de Cary, and see how he was advancing—or failing to advance—in Duke Richard's court.

Friday had come and gone without a wedding as Lucianna continued to refuse Sir Balduin's attempts to reconcile. No doubt Triston hoped to turn Sir Balduin's thoughts away from his wounded heart back to the martial pursuits that had dominated nearly the entire arc of his life. He had trained hard through his years as a squire until Triston's father, only a few years older than Sir Balduin, had dubbed him a knight at twenty-one, and in return for that boon, Sir Balduin had served Sir Damien de Brielle faithfully. He had fought beside him in every skirmish and war, whether with Sir Damien's neighbors or in the royal brawls between King Henry of England and the French. He had drilled Sir Damien's knights with efficiency and precision. And he had trained Sir Damien's sons Triston and Etienne to wield their swords skillfully and boldly, until the crippling blow at the Battle of Taillebourg had laid Sir Balduin up so long that Triston had been forced to hire a new sword master for Vere.

Triston still had confidence in Sir Balduin's judgment and eye for proficiency in the battle arts, though, and hence trusted him to return an accurate account of young Acelet's progress with the sword. Sir Balduin knew it did not bode well for a positive report when a servant at the ducal palace directed him, not to the training field where Duke Richard's squires drilled, but to the "entertainment" taking place in the great hall of the palace.

Duke Richard Plantagenet had taken Acelet under his own tutelage after the young man had rescued the honor of the de Brielle house with a surprising victory against an older and better skilled accuser in a one-on-one challenge. Sir Balduin sent a swift, worried glance around the hall, but the volatile-tempered duke appeared to be absent. Much of his court, however, stood or sat enraptured while a lithely built young man sat on the step of the dais, singing a haunting melody of a betrayed water nymph in a tenor voice so true and sweet that even Sir Balduin's pragmatic nature paused to listen in admiration.

When the last dulcet vibration of Acelet's voice finally faded away, Sir Balduin shook himself from the spell and began to maneuver himself through the crowd of listeners. He reached the dais in time to hear the collective dreamy sighs of the women gathered nearest to the singer and observe the lovesick gazes they fixed on the flaxen-haired young man. Sir Balduin remembered the girl with the shining brown hair and soft, doe-like eyes who sighed the loudest and won a somewhat hazy smile from Acelet. Linnet, Lisette — her name had been something of that sort, but Sir Balduin knew nothing of her beyond the memory of a budding affection Acelet had shown towards her while recovering from a wound incurred during the challenge that had won him Duke Richard's patronage.

It appeared to take Acelet a few moments to come completely back to earth from his song. Sir Balduin crossed his arms and tapped his toe while he waited. He still wondered if it were more luck than skill that had won Acelet's battle, for prior to that day, the boy had been annoyingly ramshackle about his training, despite his avowed desire to become a knight.

Acelet at last cast a gaze around his audience and caught Sir Balduin's eye. His fair cheeks reddened, causing Sir Balduin to realize that he was frowning at the youth. Acelet stood up, made an undeniably graceful bow coupled with a very pretty speech of thanks for the audience's attention, then excused himself, stepped down off the dais, and came to Sir Balduin's side.

"I'm not shirking my practice," Acelet said, before Sir Balduin could even greet him. "I tumbled Lucas off his horse this morning with my lance and knocked Conrad down with my staff. Sir Aigar says I am his swiftest student and had no objection to my spending the afternoon with my music. Triston said—"

"That you might pursue both interests until you made up your mind whether you'd rather be a knight or a troubadour," Sir Balduin finished, aware of his young master's bargain with his cousin.

Sir Balduin's soldier's heart could scarce conceive of anything more ridiculous than the latter choice for a young man as nobly born as Acelet. He set a hand to the young man's shoulder and steered him through the crowd to a corner of the hall where they could converse in private. Before today, Sir Balduin would have scorned the languishing gazes the women sent after them, but the emerald ring that still burned its rejection against his breast where it hung within his shirt on a chain curbed the belittling comment on his tongue. Nevertheless, his forbidding gaze caused the women to disperse so that he and Acelet reached a bench set out between the tapestries of a hunting and hawking scene with a sufficient degree of seclusion.

"Sit," Sir Balduin bade the young man, "and tell me how you fare here in Duke Richard's court."

Acelet waited until Sir Balduin sat down beside him, reluctant, perhaps, to answer from a position that set him at a disadvantage to the older man's height.

"Sir Aigar praises my speed and the accuracy of my strikes at practice," Acelet said. "Once a week, Duke Richard himself comes to watch us. He laughed when I disarmed Lucas with a maneuver he did not expect yesterday, especially when it made Lucas growl at me like a wolf deprived of his supper. At least, that's how Conrad described it. I've never heard a wolf growl, have you? I suppose it can't sound much different than an angry hound."

Sir Balduin again quelled his impatience, but made another mental note for Triston. A knight must not allow his mind to wander the way Acelet's rambling statements reflected. Sir Balduin half-wondered if Acelet had made up the story of knocking another squire down just to impress his cousin.

He asked, without much hope in the answer, "You are making friends here?"

Acelet had not shown himself particularly interested in exploring friendships with their neighbors near Vere beyond a conniving villain who had exploited his youthful naivety. Sir Balduin hoped he had learned a lesson from the experience in judging men more wisely.

"Lucas is always taunting me about one thing or another," Acelet said. "Conrad says he was Duke Richard's favorite squire before I came."

"This Conrad sounds like a good fellow." Sir Balduin knew how competition could heat the blood of youthful squires. If Acelet had managed to draw one of them onto his side against the taunting Lucas—

"Oh, he just says it to Lucas to annoy him. Conrad dislikes me, too. They all do, except for Jaufre and Folcaut."

Sir Balduin dealt an encouraging slap to Acelet's knee. "Well, do not take their remarks too hard. Young men can be jealous. It is best to ignore it if you can. Triston will be pleased that you have struck fellowship with at least a few of your fellow squires."

Acelet stared at him from eyes that were as blue as a summer's sky. "But I just told you I haven't. Not that I care.

They are all swaggering braggarts, though a few of them can feign a veneer of courtesy to please the ladies. But at heart they are like the duke himself, bullies and—"

"Have a care," Sir Balduin interrupted sharply. Acelet remained as dangerously rattlebrained as ever to spout such criticism of Duke Richard right under the noses of the duke's own court. Sir Balduin lowered his voice, but made sure it carried a firm chastisement. "If you've been prattling remarks like that, it's a wonder the duke has let you keep your head."

"Oh, I wouldn't say it to anyone but you and Triston anymore." Acelet looked unperturbed by the rebuke, but followed Sir Balduin's example and softened his voice. "And to Jaufre and Folcaut, but both of them agree with me, so I know I can trust them not to babble my words about."

It was not that Sir Balduin held no sympathy for Acelet's opinion of the duke. Allowed a choice, he knew that Triston would have thrown his allegiance to King Henry above his bloodthirsty sons, but circumstances had forced from Triston an oath of fealty to Duke Richard, and having so sworn, he would serve the duke faithfully to the death. And so, therefore, must every member of Triston's house, including Sir Balduin—and Acelet. Sir Balduin knew that Triston hoped the favors Duke Richard had showered on Acelet over the past year would turn the young man into a loyal, if reluctant, adherent of the duke's. Triston would be troubled to hear that instead, Acelet still denounced the duke's character with such thoughtless abandon.

"Whoever this Jaufre and Folcaut may be," Sir Balduin said, "they show you no friendship by encouraging you to disparage the duke. I trust they are not two of his knights. Such talk would be beyond deplorable from them, it would be treason."

"Oh, don't worry, you old grumbler. They're not knights, they are troubadours. They've sworn no fealty to any man, so if they wish to complain a bit over the toss of a dice, their heads are quite safe. And I am being careful to keep mine safe too, for Lisette."

64

It had never bothered Sir Balduin before that Acelet sometimes called him "old grumbler," any more than Acelet had ever objected to Sir Balduin calling him "young Acelet" when the youth was trying very hard to prove himself a man rather than a boy. But today the good-humored jibe stung. It caused Sir Balduin to reply more irritably than he might otherwise have done.

"Dicing with troubadours? Are you guzzling yourself to bed every night now, too? I suppose next you'll be brawling and wenching and—"

He broke off at the look of shock that spread across Acelet's face. Such behavior was only to be expected from young men Acelet's age, but apparently Acelet's head remained too firmly in the clouds of his own idealized concepts of chivalry to have entertained engaging in such vices himself.

"You think I would stain my honor and insult the woman I love with lewd conduct such as that?" Acelet's eyes gave an angry flash. "Just because Duke Richard countenances, nay encourages wantonness among his knights and laughs when they fall into a drunken mêlée in the middle of his hall, does not mean that I have allowed his court to corrupt me. I endure mockery from the likes of Lucas and Conrad, but I did not expect it from you."

Sir Balduin gave the boy credit for spirit. It took pluck to rebuke a man more than thirty years his senior for a perceived lack of morals.

"Of course I do not mock you," Sir Balduin said. "Your words—er, simply worried me." He would not admit to a ridiculous smart at being called "old" when he knew perfectly well that was what he was. "You are wise to hold yourself aloof from such pursuits. It will please Triston that you have not, as you say, been corrupted. I'd have a care if you've been gambling, though. The roll of the dice has started more than one man down the road to the vices you deplore."

"Gambling is in Jaufre's blood. It lost him his wife." Acelet drubbed his fingers against his knee as he spoke, a gesture, Sir

Balduin recalled, of boredom. "I don't know what he sees in the dice. I played a handful of games with him and found it tedious. He's a dashed fine troubadour, though." The drubbing stopped, Acelet's attention appearing to refocus with the shift to a more interesting subject. "He's taught me descriptions for all sorts of shades for women's eyes to use in one's poetry. I had no idea eyes came in so many variations, had you?"

"Do they?" Sir Balduin felt his fingers fall into a thrumming pattern of their own.

"Take Lisette's eyes," Acelet said. "Jaufre says I should never call them simply 'brown,' but 'honey brown.' I do not think they are golden enough to call 'honey,' but Jaufre said she would like it, and she does. It wins me her sweetest smiles when I sing of a honey-eyed damsel in one of my songs."

"Does it?" Sir Balduin tried to strike a casual attitude when everything in him went suddenly quite alert. "And how would you describe, say, a pair of green eyes?"

Acelet thought for a moment. "It depends on the shade, of course, but one could use grass green or forest green or leaf green or sea green. And there are always the jewel tones, like emerald or jade. Women like their eyes compared to jewels."

Sir Balduin had always thought Lucianna's eyes reminded him of emeralds. It had brought him the greatest pleasure the day he had placed his ring on her finger that its stone precisely matched her eyes.

"Are there poetic words for women's hair color, too?" he asked.

"Oh, certainly, as many or more than there are for eyes. Take Lisette—"

"What about a redhead?" Sir Balduin held little interest in the poetic virtues of Acelet's love. Despite Lucianna's insistence that she thought Acelet and his songs foolish, Sir Balduin had seen a dreamy glow steal into her eyes when Acelet had sung for them all at Christmas dinner.

"Redheads?" Again Acelet took time to reflect. "Well, there's 'copper' and 'auburn' and 'ginger' —"

"Auburn," Sir Balduin murmured. He had heard Siri call Lucianna's hair "auburn."

"Just don't call it 'foxy,'" Acelet warned, apparently too lost in thought to hear him. "'Foxy' is considered an insult, though I think the coat of a red fox is beautiful. But women don't like it, so it's best to stick to the other names."

Sir Balduin followed Acelet's gaze to where it drifted across the hall and came to rest on the girl with the honey-brown eyes—nay, Acelet was right, they were a deeper brown than honey—and the shining brown hair Sir Balduin had preempted him from describing. Lisette stood with a woman whose own hair was concealed with a wimple, though her face appeared too youthful to be framed with a matron's headdress. The latter woman frowned as Lisette sent a shy smile at Acelet, and received a like response from the young man at Sir Balduin's side. The women hovered a sufficient distance to not overhear the men's discussion, but Lisette had clearly drawn as near as she could to retain Acelet's attention.

Acelet said he sometimes sang of honey-eyed damsels. He had expanded his repertoire since Christmas.

"Do you know any songs about red-haired, green-eyed damsels?" Again, Sir Balduin attempted to inject a mere perfunctory interest in his voice. "I may as well report your progress with your music, as well as with your sword and staff, when I return to Vere."

Acelet's eyes brightened far more at this question than they had when discussing his squire's training. Brightened for an instant anyway, before blurring as though he were slowly drifting away into some other world. After several minutes, he began to sing in those same true tones that had greeted Sir Balduin's ears when he'd entered the hall.

Six

"You have always been uncommonly stubborn," Serafino said from where he lay sprawled on his back in the flowery mead of Siri's garden. He linked his hands behind his head while he gazed up at the grey autumn clouds in the mid-morning sky.

Lucianna tried to ignore him, along with the sluggish draw of her bronze needle through her linen cloth. She had exulted in the superiority of bronze over the bone needles of her youth, until Siri had given her a silver needle one Epiphany morn in Venice. Lucianna had imagined the angels who embroidered the holy altar cloths in the celestial city must all employ needles so divine for their sacred, joyous work. Lucianna's heart had rejoiced, as well, in the few, short days she had embroidered her own humbler patterns with Siri's gift, until Serafino had made her sell the needle to pay off another of his debts and keep his tongue quiet and his existence a secret from the people Lucianna loved. She had had to tell Siri she'd lost it. So many lies.

At least this time she had managed to spite Serafino by slapping the needles back into Sir Balduin's hands. But she could not stop her heart from aching for the loss of both the gift and the giver.

Serafino gave a soft snort. Lucianna hoped he had fallen

asleep, but from the way he cursed and scrubbed at his nose, she discerned a gnat had merely flown into one of his nostrils. He sat up, sufficiently annoyed by the insect's assault to glare at his sister.

"Your lover returned this morning."

"He is not my lover." Lucianna pulled the red thread through her cloth. "Nor is he longer my affianced husband. As soon as Siri's *bambino* is born, I am returning to Venice. You may come with me, or if you fear you are no longer welcome there, you may stay here to gamble and swill and otherwise squander your misbegotten life among people who do not yet know what a scoundrel you are."

Serafino lifted one of his brows. Lucianna bit her lip. He did not need to say it for her to know the silent threat her words had roused on his tongue. She should not have told Siri of his vices. He would be angry if he knew.

He plucked some periwinkle petals from his sleeve. "Those needles would have set me up for months, that ring for more than a year. A man who can afford to lavish such gifts upon you would never notice if a needle or two went missing. The ring might be more difficult to explain, but you were ever a careless wench. You could say you misplaced it—"

"Careless only when you were near. There will be no more lies for you, Serafino. *Signor* Balduin is not rich, but even if he were, I would not marry such an insensitive brute. Not even you can make me."

"Not rich? Then how did he afford those gifts?"

Lucianna did not know the answer so she had no reply. It did not matter anyway. She would not let Serafino use her in so shameful a way again.

"Does he really think you are a lady?" Serafino asked.

Lucianna set another stitch. "It is merely a habit they all fell into calling me when I came. Siri knows the truth and has surely told *Don* Triston . . ."

She hesitated. But had Triston told Sir Balduin? Lucianna had never thought to wonder before. 'Twas true, she had not corrected the servants when they had begun calling her "Lady Lucianna." Undoubtedly they did so because of the rich gowns Siri had given her and because Lucianna held her posture so very straight, as the nuns had taught her in the convent. Her disdain for her new rural surroundings, a dismal contrast at first to the great, glittering city of Venice, had also won whispers of *haughty* among the servants. Even Sir Balduin had called her "lady" from the first. There had seemed no harm in accepting it as a title of respect in her role as Siri's companion, whose own title of *donna* had only come to her through her first marriage. But what if Sir Balduin *did* believe Lucianna was nobly born?

She reminded herself that Triston had wanted to marry Siri when he had still believed her a mere craftsman's daughter, before they had all learned of her grandfather's inheritance. Surely Sir Balduin would not have shunned Lucianna for being the daughter of an Italian merchant—had it been the truth.

"What you mean," Serafino said with a sneer in his voice, "is that Siri knows that absurd story you and your dear Elisabetta concocted."

Lucianna chided herself for trailing off and allowing him to guess at her thoughts.

"Lucianna Fabio," he taunted, "orphaned daughter of Panfilo Fabio and Rosaria Piccoli, a respected merchant family from Tuscany. Struck down by an illness while in Venice where they had traveled with their new *bambina* to conduct some business, they had the forethought to cast you on the mercies of the sisters of the *convento di Santa Caterina* to raise, along with leaving you a modest dowry for a future marriage." He swatted a gnat on the back of his hand. "Not enough for a grand match, but sufficient to win the consent of Vincenzo Mirolli's father for you to wed him, *si*? Did Elisabetta's father ever learn that his daughter sold that fine pearl necklace he gave her to fabricate a dowry for you?"

Lucianna felt her cheeks grow hot, anger struggling with shame for dominance in her breast. "You know he did not, for you could never have blackmailed me all those years if he had known."

"*Si*," Serafino said. "Cosimo Gallo would have thrown you out on the streets if he'd known, instead of embracing you to his bosom as his beloved daughter's *amica cara*."

Lucianna set a line of stitches in rigid silence. To speak would only encourage Serafino's gibes. It had seemed a harmless enough ruse when she and Elisabetta Gallo had invented the story they told Elisabetta's father. They had had years to weave an elaborate, convincing, and tragic tale of Lucianna's unknown parentage. Two young girls who had become inseparable during their time in the abbey, desperate and determined to maintain their sisterhood when Elisabetta's father finally called her home.

Lucianna had sought so hard to resign herself to eventually joining the nuns' order, for what other future could there be for a poor foundling babe left upon the abbey's doorstep? But as Elisabetta blossomed and began to speak eagerly of marriage, Lucianna had found herself dreaming, too. And then Elisabetta, passionate, impulsive Elisabetta had struck upon the plan. Oh, the lies they had told to her father and the nuns, each behind the other's backs, to persuade the merchant that Lucianna held such birth as to make her worthy of Cosimo's compassion to take her into his home with his daughter, and convince the nuns that the merchant had taken pity on a foundling girl to adopt her for his daughter's sake. How many times Lucianna had held her breath in terror that they would be exposed, but Elisabetta, clever as well as passionate, had somehow managed to keep her father and the nuns befuddled to their strategy until Lucianna stood safely beneath Cosimo Gallo's roof.

"Elisabetta," Lucianna whispered. "*Mia amica cara*."

What wild, exciting days had followed as Lucianna found herself courted by nearly as many men as Elisabetta, though none of them as rich as her friend's suitors. But thanks to the pearl necklace Elisabetta had sold, handsome, charming

Vincenzo Mirolli had asked for Lucianna's hand before her sixteenth year. And then—then Serafino, the brother she had never known she had, suddenly appeared and ruined everything.

Just as he had once more materialized as if from a nightmare and had spoiled everything again.

"Why do you stay?" Lucianna asked crossly. "I will not change my mind about *Signor* Balduin. Go back to Venice. I will join you there when Siri's *bambino* is born."

Serafino's lip curled. "And what will you do in Venice, *cara*? You have no home to go to. You were always dependent on Elisabetta and her children to give you a roof over your head, and Lady Siri's roof is now here in Poitou."

"I will join the sisters of the *convento di Santa Caterina*. If I had known of your despicable existence, I would never have left there." Oh, how it chilled her to say it. But she could see no other way.

"But *no*, you were in a glow when I first laid eyes on you, laughing and flirting and dancing as lightly as a fairy while the men around you basked in the fiery rays of your luster. You were not meant for abstinence and prayers, but for a life overflowing with love. All these years you have done naught but spite yourself by denying the cravings of your heart. No husband, no children—it did not need to be so, *cara*."

"You gave me no choice." Bitterness made her jerk the thread so tight it puckered the cloth. She sought to smooth it out with a hand that trembled slightly. "If I had married Vincenzo, he would have come to hate me."

"He hated you anyway."

"*Si*, thanks to you, but only for a day, a week, a month perhaps—but not for a lifetime. He married Agata di Luzio and forgot all about me." At least, Lucianna prayed he had.

Serafino's threat, one he had vindictively fulfilled, had robbed her of a husband and family, as he had said, but she had shared in the love of Elisabetta's children and cherished them as her own. Unlike Vincenzo, dear Elisabetta had remained true to her friendship with Lucianna when Serafino had shocked them both with the truth.

Elisabetta had dashed her father's high hopes for her and eloped with an illuminator from Poitou who had abandoned his pilgrimage to the Holy Land when he fell in love with her. Inseparable as always from the bond of their youth, Elisabetta had taken Lucianna with her into the new home she established with her husband in Venice, one that, though comfortable, was humbler than the merchant's house she had left. It had made paying off Serafino's repeated demands for silence more difficult, but they had had no choice. Having exposed her once before, neither of the women had doubted that he would do so again to Elisabetta's new husband, who might take the news as ill as Vincenzo had and seek to turn Lucianna out of his house and eliminate her influence over his children.

Lucianna had embroidered her fingers numb and sold her work to earn enough coins to make Serafino go away again and again. When his debts and demands grew higher than she could meet, Elisabetta surreptitiously sold some of her husband's paints to meet the difference, telling her husband she had clumsily spilled them, knowing he adored her too much to even scold.

Lucianna knew then, as she knew now, that she should have had more courage. She should have put a stop to it by telling Elisabetta's husband and everyone else the truth, even if it had meant the joyous life she had found outside the convent walls must be snuffed by embracing that abstinent life of prayer that Serafino described and which Lucianna still knew so ill-fitted her.

But she was no longer the frightened girl she had been when Serafino had first revealed himself to her, or the proud young woman who could not bear for the world to know the shame of the truth, or the zealous adoptive mother whose heart would break if Siri had been ripped from her arms after Elisabetta's death. Siri was wed and happy now, with the experience of years to sustain her through her future, unlike the naïve sixteen-year-old she had been at her first marriage. Much as Lucianna would like to have enjoyed sharing Siri's motherhood, as she had Elisabetta's, she knew herself no longer truly needed. Serafino could only hurt her most deeply now if she stayed.

A dark-haired serving girl slipped into the garden. She dipped a curtsy to Lucianna. "The trenchers are being laid in the hall," she said. "May I help you change your gown for dinner, milady?"

Serafino arced a satirical brow at the deferential address, but Lucianna ignored him and neatly folded her embroidery.

"*Si, grazie,* Audiart. I shall wear the cream colored surcote with the yellow sunbursts on the bodice. Was it laundered as I requested?"

The serving girl frowned a little. "Yes, milady, but are you sure—?"

"And the amber necklace," Lucianna finished. She tucked her cloth in her workbasket, rose with the basket in her hands, and said crisply, "Come!" to the servant.

Though her brother's taste in clothes was extravagant, his eye always focused on the richness of the cloth, value of the jewels or the extravagance of the embroidery, not whether any of these flattered the wearer or not. So he would not guess that she had deliberately chosen for her dining attire colors that would wash out her complexion and allow all the flaws of her forty-four year old face to shine through.

The others were gathered in the hall by the time Lucianna joined them. Siri had used her new found wealth to create small changes in the modest hall: new tapestries on the walls so that she could move the boating scene to her workshop; lavender sprinkled among the rushes; and a small ensemble of musicians, already playing their viols and recorder beneath the hubbub of the hungry, waiting household. A fire had been set in the stone hearth near the kitchen exit, too far away to truly warm the diners, but casting a glow of heat about Lucianna as she walked past it.

Triston and Siri sat at the center of the white clothed table on the dais, with the banner of Triston's house—the five-petaled gilded rose with a blood red center—flowing down the wall behind them. Sir Balduin sat to Triston's right, and next to him stood the empty chair waiting for Lucianna. She regretted the day she had agreed to rearrange her position to sit beside Sir Balduin rather than at Siri's side. Serafino now sat in Lucianna's former place, attempting to charm his hostess, judging from the angelic grin accompanying his conversation with Siri. Siri appeared to be responding with a distant politeness. Was she remembering Luicianna's revelations of Serafino's character? Lucianna prayed for Siri's discretion.

Serafino's gaze shifted to his sister as Lucianna approached the dais but his eyes held no accusation, only a familiar calculation. His gaze slid from her to Sir Balduin. Despite her challenge in the garden, she knew Serafino lingered at Vere because he still hoped she would change her mind about wedding the knight.

Lucianna ignored Sir Balduin's tentative smile as she stepped to his side and sniffed one of her disdainful sniffs, loudly enough to proclaim her displeasure as she sank into her chair. She kept her gaze strictly fixed on the tables below the dais where the rest of the household knights and men-at-arms dined. It required a powerful exertion of will, for her eyes longed to drift to the face of the man who sighed rather dispiritedly beside her, starved for his features after his week-long absence from Vere Castle.

As soon as Father Michel pronounced grace and the musicians renewed their quiet strains, Siri leaned away from Serafino to address Sir Balduin. "And so you must tell us, sir, how you found Acelet at court. Is he well? Does he seem happy there?"

"At first, I thought him little changed," Sir Balduin replied. "His head is still too much in the clouds, in my opinion. He squanders a great deal of his free time among Duke Richard's troubadours and jongleurs. One day he sat in the gardens for hours, thinking only of how to perfect a single rhyme. Or at least, 'twas the only task he appeared to be engaged in each time I entered the gardens that day to speak with him. He told me I must go away until he solved the riddle of his words, for I distracted him and he could not focus on my questions while the mystery buzzed like a bee in his head."

Little changed indeed, Lucianna thought, the foolish boy. Her tongue tanged at the aromas that wafted down the table as servants began to appear with their savory offerings. She sensed Sir Balduin's nod beside her, signifying his desire for the gilded chicken one of them placed upon his trencher. In general, their tastes were very similar, but Lucianna allowed the selection to pass by her and chose some duck with chawdon sauce, instead.

"He has abandoned all interest in a knighthood, then?" Triston asked of his young cousin.

Lucianna could not quite tell whether the note in his voice suggested disapproval or hope. She was tempted to glance at Triston to search his expression, but she would have to look past Sir Balduin and feared her gaze would go no further.

"I feared 'twas the case." There was no misinterpreting the disapproval in Sir Balduin's voice. Lucianna knew his various inflections too well to mistake. "But then I saw him at his sword practice, and it was just as he told me the day I arrived. Yes, thank you, some of that salt cod, please."

Lucianna chose the pike in rosemary sauce. Did she catch another sigh from Sir Balduin before he continued his remarks to Triston?

"I thought he was boasting so that I would bring you a fair report, lest you say he was wasting the duke's time and drag him back to Vere, or worse, send him home to his father. But to my surprise, he'd spoken truly. He was not like his days here, when he fought like a lion when he fought at a shadow, but shrank from the blows of the sword master's thrusts."

It became too much. Lucianna allowed herself a glance at Sir Balduin's hands, trusting his preoccupation with Triston to deflect him from her awareness of him. He was twirling his dining knife as he often did when distracted with conversation while dining. She expected to see the emerald ring she had returned upon his finger, but his strong, brown hands bore only the humble amethyst and garnet rings he claimed had been awarded him years ago by Triston's father. What had he done with the emerald?

"While I stood watching," his deep, familiar tones rolled on, "Acelet knocked the other squires down, every one, with both his sword and staff. He is not always so sure on horseback yet. He confessed to me in that naïve way of his that the cadence of the horse's paces sometimes drifts his mind into melody — aye, sir, absurd! But that is Acelet for you."

Another servant appeared at Sir Balduin's shoulder. Lucianna snapped her attention back to her trencher. She was preparing herself to allow this dish to pass by her too and once more select the opposite of Sir Balduin's choice, when she heard him exclaim with delight.

"A hodgepodge! I see Lady Lucianna has been in the kitchens again."

That finally startled her into glancing full into his beaming face before dropping her gaze to the golden browned goose covered with a thick, savory sauce being served onto Sir Balduin's trencher. Prior to her arrival at Vere, the castle's cook made the sauce with ginger and a little cider vinegar. Lucianna had indeed added her own touch to the dish by replacing the cider with wine and adding cloves and mace, both of which spices drifted from Sir Balduin's trencher to her nose. The new recipe had seduced Sir Balduin's hearty appetite and quickly become his favorite dish.

Lucianna shot a glance down the table at Siri, who avoided her gaze so carefully that Lucianna was certain Siri had ordered the dish to be served. Siri had said she would not try to change Lucianna's mind about Sir Balduin, but if a hodgepodge on his trencher gave him hope that Lucianna was having second thoughts and encouraged him to try to change her mind himself, Siri likely thought her conscience at quits.

Lucianna started to deny that she had had anything to do with the dish, but Sir Balduin preempted her with a robust smacking of his lips that followed the morsel of sauce-dripping goose he popped into his mouth, chewed and swallowed.

"Delicious!" he pronounced. "Nothing I ate in the duke's court tasted half so fine as this. My thanks to you, Lady Lucianna. Why, I cannot think of anything that could cheer a man more than a warm, savory dish of hodgepodge after a brisk, autumn day's journey."

The jauntiness in his voice alarmed her, for it bespoke the very emotion she wished to quell. "But I did not—"

Another contented swallow and smack cut her off, then he addressed Triston again with a smile too jovial for her comfort.

"Why, I nearly forgot, sir. I told Acelet I would share one of his new songs with you. So that you might judge whether his talent has progressed as far in his music as it has with sword and staff. Shall I—er, may I do so now?"

Sir Balduin to share a song? Lucianna gazed at him in astonishment. Or rather, she stared at the grey ripples on the back of his head, for his own gaze remained fixed on Triston. The amazement on Triston's and Siri's faces surely matched Lucianna's own, but after a startled pause, Triston said, "Why, certainly."

Sir Balduin laid down his knife, the blade swimming in the hodgepodge sauce, took a long drink from his wine goblet, then stood up. A motion from his hand quieted the musicians. His cheeks tinged faintly pink. He drew a long breath, then began to sing.

I saw her late on an autumn day,
> "Bathed in the glory of the sun at its setting."

Yes, he was sure those were the words Acelet had taught him. Sir Balduin felt fairly certain of the tune. Though he did not consider himself a man of music, tunes usually stuck in his head. Poetry, like Italian, dismayed him, though, making him question his wits when he faltered, upsetting the confidence in his intelligence that he realized he'd always taken for granted in plainspoken conversations. But he had let Acelet drill him on these lines over two dozen times.

"She sat beneath the great oak tree,
"Head cocked to catch the robin's song that had not yet faded . . . "

He and Acelet had argued over which bird to use. Acelet said nightingales were more romantic, even though it was unlikely for one to be singing in the autumn at dusk. Sir Balduin's practical mind had insisted on the robin.

"And so to skyward sent I this plea
"To the melancholy fowl — "

No, that was not right. He paused, then re-sang the scale.

"To the melancholy cock — "

Had it been a cock? Well, it would have to do, he would not embarrass himself by singing the phrase a third time.

" — who held her ear,

"That it might carry these words to her heart."

He chanced a glance at Lucianna then. The musicians, catching onto the tune, inserted a soft interlude during his pause. Did she think him a fool to stand here, singing to the company thus? The company surely must. His cheeks warmed at the thought, but if it pleased her, he would bear the humiliation. She looked more sallow than usual, though he was not sure why. Perhaps it was something about the wan gown she wore that failed to flatter a complexion that could put younger women to shame for its smoothness. True, a few lines webbed the corners of her eyes and tickled across her high brow, and shadows stood out beneath her eyes, shadows that he vaguely recalled faded when she wore gowns of green or blue. But nothing could rob the brilliant color of her eyes, or dim the glow that nested in them — a glow he had seen steal there whenever Acelet sang, despite her swift dismissal of both poetry and poet when the melodies came to an end.

And so Sir Balduin bolstered himself to sing on boldly.

"'Fair donna,' sang the robin — "

Would it please her to insert an Italian word? One of the few he could remember.

"' — gentle lady, the knight who worships you

"'Bids me bear to you this news,

"'That he neither eats nor sleeps for thought of you

"'Since that cruel day when you sent him away in your pride.

"'He lies upon his bed watching the moon inch across its purple canopy — "

Had it been inch or creep? And had the canopy been purple? Perhaps it had been plum. Or maybe indigo? He scrambled for the next note.

"'The sun rises upon eyes rimmed red with his night's long wakefulness.

"'When his squire begs him to break his fast, he groans.

"'As well ask him to eat ashes as find pleasure in the sweet meats of his cook."

Did he mistake, or did a twitch of a smile soften the corners of Lucianna's mouth? He sang hopefully on.

"'In waking dreams he sees naught but your foxy hair – '"

Lucianna's nose wrinkled, as though in distaste. Oh, dear. Had the word not been foxy? But he quite well remembered Acelet praising the color of the fox's fur. What was the correct word then for the pretty reddish-brown shade of her hair that strayed from beneath her veil? He hurried on to her eyes.

"'And basks in the memory of when your eyes embraced him

"'Like a sun kissed pool of emeralds.'"

Sir Balduin halted so abruptly the musicians rushed awkwardly to fill his break. That last phrase had sounded well in his head, but felt terribly wrong when it fell from his tongue. What was it Acelet had told him to sing again? Something about sea green eyes. He had been quite insistent on it, for he said it better matched the rhythm of the song, but Sir Balduin had argued doggedly for emeralds until Acelet had sighed and altered the line. Sir Balduin realized he had confused the two versions, morphing them into a simile that startled snickers from the company below the dais. Even he knew that emeralds did not come in "pools." The laughter heated his face, but what panicked him was the dismay in the green eyes he had sought to praise. Alarm at Lucianna's apparent consternation tumbled his next words into a complete muddle, and for the first time, he felt his notes veer wildly out of tune.

"'Your swan white cheeks – '"

Or was that her neck?

"' – with their cherry blush – '"

Oh, blazes. Cherry should have described her lips!

"' – the flutter of your auburn lashes – '"

Auburn! Not foxy, for her hair!

"' – and your milky smile – '"

Milky? Nay, it should have been milk white and referred to her teeth. Why had he not heeded Acelet's first suggestion to compare them to ivory?

The company was chortling loudly now. A quick glance down the great table revealed even Siri biting down on a quivering lip, while Triston stared at Sir Balduin as though a stranger had taken his place on the dais.

"Oh!" Lucianna's cry brought Sir Balduin's gaze back to her face. "You are drunk!"

All melody evaporated from his soul. "I am not—" he began with some indignation, but she sprang up from her chair and slapped her hands against his chest, so startling him that he stepped back and collided with the armrest of Triston's chair, throwing him into a slight stumble.

"As I said. Drunk!"

He followed her own glance down the table to where she met her brother's eyes. Serafino sat with a hand over his mouth, no doubt to hide his laughter. Sir Balduin cursed himself roundly for his stupidity. She would never forgive him for humiliating her in front of her kin. Any hope that he might successfully disclaim that his poem had anything to do with Lucianna was dashed when her eyes snapped back to him with a glittering glare.

"Foxy hair? Milky smile? You are not only drunk, you are an atrociously bad poet. And emeralds do not come in pools!" She swept away from him to pause between Siri and Serafino. "You ask a great deal of me, *carissima*, to expect me to endure another month of such lamentable attention. I do not know that I can bear it, truly I do not!"

Siri jumped up to catch her arm as Lucianna started to leave the dais. "Lucianna, wait! I am certain Sir Balduin did not mean to insult you. It is—it is a misunderstanding, merely. You have only to look at him to see his chagrin."

Aye, look at me, the silent plea pounded in his breast. *Look and see how I love you and how you will take springtime from my heart if you go away.*

Lucianna glanced at him with obvious reluctance. Something flickered in the emerald depths he had sought so clumsily to praise. For a moment he thought the glitter softened and felt a stir of hope, but she quenched it with the scornful tones of her reply.

"He cannot beguile his way back into my favor merely because he has shown himself a brave and loyal soldier, offers me silver needles that glide through cloth as smoothly as a lover's kiss, and has a singing voice fine enough to charm away a woman's senses. *No,* I will endure no more of his discourtesies and affronts. Unless he agrees to absent himself from the table, I will take my meals in my room after this."

He cannot beguile his way back into my favor thudded between Sir Balduin's ears as she stepped off the dais, her formerly pale cheeks ablaze at the laughter that followed her out of the hall. He stood, hope replaced with a plunging despair, until Siri's gaze captured his, urgent and compelling. *Go after her.* He prayed he read the message aright. Siri knew Lucianna better than anyone. He dodged around Triston's chair but before he could round the table, Serafino surged up from his place and blocked his path.

"Ah, *signore,* I think it is time that you and I speak. You insult my sister on the one hand and continue to pursue her on the other. I cannot see her wed to a buffoon."

Sir Balduin's own face flamed again as a shard of fresh hurt lodged in his breast. She had called him selfish, inconsiderate, disrespectful and vain. But a buffoon? No woman would happily marry a man she viewed as a fool, a man the entire castle laughed at, though the roar of hilarity had begun to subside, doused by Triston's glare at the men who depended on his good will. Instead of winning Lucianna back with a song meant to bespeak his adoration, Sir Balduin had made himself so contemptible to her that he had likely annihilated his last chance with her.

Serafino startled him by laying a hand on his shoulder and continuing with an unexpected smile, "But perhaps, as *Donna* Siri says, this is merely a misunderstanding. Let us speak in someplace private, you and I, so that we may come to know one another. Convince me that you are worthy of my sister's hand, and I may be persuaded to intercede with her on your behalf."

Sir Balduin did not see how he could redeem himself after this disaster, yet he could not prevent the return of a fresh flutter of hope at Serafino's words. If anyone could persuade Lucianna to forgive him, surely it would be her own brother? He glanced at Triston and won his nod of permission to leave the hall. Siri had returned to her chair with her pretty lips frowning. No doubt she thought Sir Balduin should follow Lucianna instead, but surely it would be better to win her brother's favor first?

"The garden," Sir Balduin said. "It will be empty this time of day." Unless Lucianna had sought refuge there with her ever-present embroidery. But that, he was certain, was one hope too many.

It was. However, the garden was not empty, as Sir Balduin had predicted. Triston's eight-year-old son, Perrin, was there, doing battle against a rose bush with his wooden sword. Despite its blunted edge, the boy severed several crisp red flowers from their stems, sending them flying like tiny heads through the air. The boy turned to stare at the two men as they joined him.

"Perrin," Sir Balduin said, "it is not the hour for your sword practice. Should you not be studying your lessons for Father Michel?" Both the sword master and the chaplain, Sir Balduin knew, were still eating in the hall. Perrin should have finished his own midday meal a good hour ago.

"I wrote out all the Latin lines he gave me," Perrin replied, "and added all my sums twice to be sure they were right. Then I went to Siri's workshop to finish my painting there, but she is out of green paint. I would have used the red, but I know she is using it for Lady Lucianna's wedding gift. I thought Siri might not want me to use it up, and the other colors looked boring today, so I brought my sword out to the garden until everyone is finished dining." His vivid blue gaze weighed Serafino with curiosity. "Are you Lady Lucianna's brother?" he asked. "Your hair is almost the same color as hers."

So, the boy had not been introduced to Serafino?

"Aye," Sir Balduin said, "this is Serafino Fabio. He is from Venice, like Lady Siri and Lady Lucianna, and has come to visit his sister." And possibly carry her back to their Italian home. Sir Balduin must send the boy away so that he could convince Serafino to stand his ally instead.

Perrin tilted his dark, curly head to one side, still studying the man at Sir Balduin's side. "Siri said she did not want me to meet you, but she did not tell me why." He shifted his gaze to Sir Balduin, as though expecting him to explain.

The pronouncement took Sir Balduin aback. He cast a startled look at Serafino and saw the reddish brows twitch briefly down before smoothing out with an accompanying easy smile.

"Women are mystifying creatures, who sometimes take odd fantasies in their heads," Serafino said. "A boy as handsome as you will learn that for yourself one day." When Perrin looked unsatisfied, he added a playful laugh to his smile. "Oh, it is likely my addiction to dice that she fears I might afflict you with. I have a bit of a fire for it in my blood, I regret to confess, but I would never corrupt a child with the vice. Women, though, can be a bit overprotective. So you had best run along and keep to yourself that you met me here in the garden."

Sir Balduin nodded his agreement at the boy, adding a bit of sternness to the gesture, for the sooner he could get Serafino alone, the sooner he might find a way to win back Lucianna.

Perrin sighed, but he gave Sir Balduin and Serafino each a neat little bow, and obediently traipsed back to the castle

"A rather impertinent whelp," Serafino muttered when he was gone. Then he whirled abruptly to clap Sir Balduin on the shoulder and asked with a return of his jaunty grin, "And so, *signore*, you must tell me, how long have you been in love with my sister?"

Sir Balduin inwardly recoiled from the bald question. His nature among strangers was generally reserved, and despite Serafino's kinship to Lucianna, he was still more stranger than not to Sir Balduin. He did not find it easy to lay his emotions open until he achieved some level of familiarity with a person, which was why it had taken him so long to nervously declare his affection to Lucianna. Only desperation had driven him to risk the inner privacy he held so dear with that debacle of a song before Triston's entire household.

He answered now, rather stiffly. "She charmed me from the moment she crossed the castle's threshold."

Charmed? Perhaps intrigued would have been a more accurate word, for Lucianna's high dignity, proud manners, and open disdain for her new home had at first been more intimidating than charming. Yet she had appropriated every previously idle thought in Sir Balduin's head almost from the first.

"*Si,*" Serafino said, "well, that is no surprise. She has always been very *bella*. Men swarmed to her twenty-nine years ago." He dug an elbow into Sir Balduin's ribs, his green eyes, so like Lucianna's, gleaming slyly. "There may be a few — let us say, crinkles — to her face now that were not there then, but her figure is still buxom enough to tempt a saint, eh?"

Bella. Sir Balduin knew that meant pretty, while her figure, though trim, was undeniably curvy. Sir Balduin could not deny that he found her physically attractive. But it was her tigress nature he had come to love, once he had realized it stemmed not from dignity or pride or disdain as had first appeared, but from a fierce protectiveness for those she cherished with a dauntless passion. She loved Siri with such vehemence. Sir Balduin had dared to hope she might learn to love him thus, too, but after today —

Despair overcame his constraint. He sank down with a groan on one of the low wattle walls that enclosed the garden and dropped his head into his hands. "What have I done? I have humiliated her beyond forgiveness with that blunder of a song."

"Now, now," Serafino said, his cheerful tones colliding against Sir Balduin's wretchedness. "Women are whimsical creatures, one day a termagant, the next day a kitten. Lucianna is temperamental, but she has always given fair ear to my counsel. The question is, are you worth me making her purr for you again? What have you to offer her, *signore*, besides a fine singing voice?"

Sir Balduin straightened, stung by what could only be words of mockery. "I may be an abysmal poet, but I offer her an honest and devoted heart."

"Oh, *si*, I do not doubt that, but a woman like my sister requires more. Forgive me, *signore*, for being frank, but you are some years her senior and women who reach her age often outlive their husbands by a considerable number of years. It would be irresponsible of me not to worry for her welfare after you are gone."

"Gone?" Sir Balduin surged to his feet. "You mean dead? I am perfectly healthy, sir, save for this limp. My father lived a good long life, more than a score of years older than I am now. I trust I shall care well for your sister for many years to come."

"Well, but the future can be unpredictable, *signore*. You might live to the outlandish age of eighty, or you might drop dead on your wedding night. What support would you leave her beyond that handsome emerald ring she threw back in your face and a set of silver embroidery needles?"

Discussing the possibility of his death struck Sir Balduin as disturbing and distasteful, but he could not entirely argue with Serafino's logic. Because Sir Balduin's father survived just short of seventy-five years did not guarantee his son would do the same. As he reflected back on the fifty-two years he had lived thus far, he realized they appeared from today's vantage to have gone by very fast. How swiftly might fly a mere twenty more?

The thought left him somewhat shaken.

"You have no lands of your own," Serafino's voice broke in jarringly, "or you would not be in another man's service. And yet poor men cannot afford emerald rings and silver needles. You will forgive me, *signore*, for being somewhat puzzled at your status."

"The ring was my grandmother's," Sir Balduin said. "She left it to me at her death." No matter what his straits through the years, he could never bring himself to part with it. "Lord Triston gave me an advance on the wages I will earn when he makes me castellan of Dauvillier Castle to buy the needles."

"I see." Serafino rubbed his thumb across his lower lip. "Castellan, eh? How big is this castle *Don* Triston means to entrust to you? What is the wage he has promised? My sister has been generously cared for by *Donna* Siri. I do not think I could consent to see her dress or eat less finely than she did in Venice or does here at Vere. Perhaps you have more of your grandmother's jewels than that emerald ring, eh? It would ease my mind, you understand, if you had some independent wealth to leave her, for *Don* Triston will surely displace her with another castellan and his wife when you die, and what shall become of her then?"

Sir Balduin stood disconcerted before this flurry of questions. He had no independent wealth, nor ever would. But he could not simply conceded defeat because of that.

Before he could gather a defense for Lucianna's hand, Serafino flashed a blinding smile, then to Sir Balduin's surprise, pulled him into a sudden embrace, thumping him on the back as though they were bosom friends.

"Fair concerns for a loving brother, *si?*" he said, his voice ringing in Sir Balduin's ear. Another thump before he stood away. "*Scusi!* I see I startled you. It is our way between *amici* in Venice — how would you say it? — friends, and you and I may soon be *cognato* — brothers-by-marriage, *si?* Come, *signore*, let us sit together." Serafino dropped down in a negligent posture on the wattle wall. "Tell me all you can offer her and I will have her back in your arms in no time."

III

The Piazza San Marco ~ Venice 1152

*L*ucianna *bounced excitedly on the tips of her toes. Panfilo. I know* it will say Panfilo. *Elisabetta touched her arm, as if in caution, but Lucianna gave her no heed. Elisabetta had been suspicious from the first moment that Serafino, the woolmonger's son, had drawn them aside in her father's hall after conducting some business with Cosimo Gallo on behalf of Serafino's father, Domenico Amorosi.*

"I knew your father," Serafino whispered to Lucianna, with Elisabetta standing close enough to hear. "Meet me on the Piazza San Marco just after noon tomorrow and I will show you his name."

Lucianna caught Elisabetta by the hands, stunned as Serafino strode away from them. "Elisabetta — my father!" She had waited all her life for the news Serafino promised.

Elisabetta gazed after him. "I do not trust him," she murmured. "He and Domenico sell wool to my father to be woven into cloth, but there is something about Serafino that sets my skin a-crawl."

"Oh, but that is absurd. Did you not see how he smiled? As beautiful as an angel. So lovely a smile as that cannot mean us harm. He did not ask to meet us in some dark corner, but in the middle of the busiest square in Venice."

"I did not like him," Elisabetta repeated. "There is something . . ."

She trailed off, but Lucianna caught the way she glanced at Lucianna's hair. Lucianna had drawn back the sides of her thick auburn locks and plaited them in a braid down her back. It was not a common color, she knew, but neither was it so rare as to make her question the similar shade of Serafino's hair. His eyes were green like hers, too, but she had met others with green eyes since leaving the convent to live with Elisabetta and her father in the grand house the merchant had built with his lifetime's accumulated wealth.

Despite her doubts, Elisabetta agreed to accompany Lucianna to the designated meeting place. People milled around them, streaming in and out of the beautiful five domed cathedral basilica, traveling to or from the doge's palace, or merely gathering to conduct business or gossip. Lucianna shaded her eyes from the sun with her hand and gazed this way and that, wondering from which direction Serafino would approach them. What was taking him so long?

And then she saw him, wearing a cap on his head at a tilted, rakish angle. She had noticed yesterday that its feather had looked worn, as had his tunic, while her keen seamstress's eye had noted the hole cursorily darned in his hose over one of his knees.

He bowed to them as he reached them, with a grace that more nearly reflected his name than his tired clothing. "Signorine. My thanks for your patience. It took me a little longer than I expected to obtain this for you."

Lucianna saw that the pretty purple amethyst ring he had worn yesterday no longer adorned the hand that held a slender parchment roll. The jewel had not suited his coloring, but then, neither did the ruby brooch that clasped her mantle at her shoulder. It had surprised her to learn that the "red stone" her parents had left with her had in fact been a ruby. No wonder the abbess had wanted it for her nun's dowry. But they had returned it to her when she left the convent with Elisabetta. Lucianna wore the brooch always, though it so ill-flattered her hair, certain it had been a gift from her unknown mother or father.

She glanced into Serafino's handsome face. His green gaze roamed over her features in such an intimate way that it heated her cheeks. She had not lacked for suitors since Cosimo had taken her into his home, all of them men of modest wealth and respectable merchant birth. The richer men courted Elisabetta, along with a number of lower but very wealthy nobles bewitched by Elisabetta's beauty and dowry. In the six months since they had left the abbey, the happiest days of Lucianna's life, Lucianna had quickly given her fifteen-year-old heart to twenty-year-old Vincenzo Mirolli, with his flamboyant tunics and hats, his resonate laughter, and his dark teasing eyes. He had asked for her hand in marriage only yesterday.

Beautiful as Serafino was, he was ten years her senior. That, and her love for Vincenzo, made her shift nervously as Serafino's gaze lingered on her face a little too long

"You said you would tell me of my father," she said, hoping to distract him from any improper amorous thoughts. Had Elisabetta's suspicions of him been correct? But they were perfectly safe, standing thus in the middle of the crowds on the piazza.

"I have it here." Serafino indicated the parchment roll. "But are you sure you wish to know?"

Lucianna stared at him, surprised. "But of course! How can you wonder?" Then she realized that he might not know the story of her past. "I am an orphan," she said, ignoring Elisabetta's warning tug on her sleeve, "left to the care of the nuns of the Convent of Saint Catherine when my parents died. All my life I have wished to know of my parents. Please, be kind and tell me quickly."

She began to bounce on her toes again, this time with impatience.

Elisabetta spoke across Lucianna's eagerness. "But first, sir, we should like to know how you know anything about them at all. You could have been naught but a boy when Lucianna came to the nuns."

Lucianna glanced at her. Did she think Serafino had fabricated a lie? Why should he do so?

Serafino hesitated. He glanced around them, waiting for a lull to appear in the crowd passing by, then reached out a finger to touch Lucianna's brooch. "I know because of this. May I?"

His motion took Lucianna so aback that he had the brooch free in his hand before she could protest.

"Give it back," Elisabetta said sharply. "It is not yours."

"No," he agreed, his gaze, like his words, still directed at Lucianna. "It is our mother's, dear one."

His statement bereft even Elisabetta of speech. He pulled free a dagger he wore, turned over the brooch, and used the blade to pry the ruby free of its setting. Then he held out the jewel to Lucianna. Someone had scratched some letters into the back. A-M-O-R . . .

"Amorosi?" she read aloud. "But that is your name."

Again he waited for a calm in the crowd before saying softly, "And our mother's by marriage. She was Antonia d'Arro before she wed, but my father gave her that brooch with her new name inscribed on their wedding day. She wore it so often when I was a boy that I recognized it as soon as I saw it on your shoulder."

He returned the disassembled brooch to Lucianna. Serafino was her brother? But . . . "You are the son of Domenico Amorosi, the woolmonger who sometimes sells his work to Cosimo Gallo." Domenico, not Panfilo?

"Yes," Serafino said. "And I stood at watch while our mother laid you on the doorstep of the convent. She kissed you, then tucked the brooch into your blanket, why, I do not know. Perhaps as payment to the nuns for their care of you."

But the nuns had not sold it. Instead they had kept it safe for Lucianna all those years. She should be elated. The mystery of her life had just been revealed! She was the daughter of Domenico and Antonia Amorosi! Woolmongery was a respectable trade and a profitable one, merchants who traveled sometimes as far afield as Flanders and England to purchase the fleece that Italian cloth makers then wove into fabrics to sell. But puzzlement bubbled within her alongside her exhilaration. Antonia was not as pretty as Rosaria, but she knew she had invented the latter name. But what, then, had her dream meant of the shining young man? Had it been nothing more than a wishful evocation from her lonely, childish heart?

Elisabetta spoke again, a small frown upon her mouth. "You are saying you are Lucianna's brother?"

That explained why Serafino's hair so nearly matched Lucianna's, and the green eyes they shared. She had never seen his father in Cosimo's house. My father, *she corrected herself with an odd, tumbling sensation in her stomach. Did he have hair like theirs, or had she inherited the color from her mother? And her eyes — were* they Antonia's or Domenico's? No wonder Serafino had studied her face so closely!

She became aware that he continued to time their conversation to those sometimes lengthy breaks among the swarms of people milling past.

"Brother, yes," Serafino said, "but" — he caught Lucianna's gaze again — "are you sure you wish to know all, dear one? I may call you that, may I not, since we share in part our blood?"

He spoke almost tenderly, as one might to a younger sister, yet she sensed a hint of caution in his voice, as well.

Her brows drew together in a pucker, puzzled by his manner. "Why do you ask me that again?" Her lashes fluttered up as the answer came to her. "Is it that our parents do not know that I am here? Do they think me in the convent still?" And then followed hard the painful realization that should have struck her as obvious from the first, had she not been so eager for Serafino's revelation. "Oh!" Her hand covered her suddenly trembling lips. "They — they did not want me, did they?"

Why else would they have abandoned her to the nuns?

Elisabetta's arm slid around her shoulders, embracing Lucianna, seeking to impart comfort to the knowledge Elisabetta must have feared as soon as Serafino approached them in her father's hall.

A gentle pity settled across Serafino's face. "If you wish it, I shall walk away without speaking any more. Return to Cosimo Gallo's house, dear one. Be Lucianna Fabio. Marry your Vincenzo and be happy. I do not wish to bring you grief."

He began to turn away, but Lucianna pulled free of Elisabetta and caught him by the arm.

"No! Why did they not want me? I wish to know!"

Serafino raised one graceful, auburn brow at her. "Do you?"

"Yes! Tell me!"

"Lucianna," Elisabetta said pleadingly, trying to pull her away.

But a resolute fire had filled Lucianna. She had spent her life in ignorance and false dreams. Now at last, bitter or sweet, she would know the truth.

She pointed at the parchment roll in Serafino's hand. "The answer is there, isn't it? What does it say?"

She grabbed it from his fist, fearful from his hesitance that he might try to deny it to her. With shaking fingers, she spread open the parchment and read. But it made no sense.

"It is a court case," she said, "for a man named Giovanni." She tilted the parchment so that Elisabetta might read the name and the details of his crime. "What does this have to do with me?"

It seemed to her that some of the gentleness left Serafino's face as she stared at him in confusion.

"Antonia Amorosi was your mother, dear one, but he" – Serafino nodded towards the parchment – "was your father."

Elisabetta's arm snaked around her shoulders again as Lucianna nearly staggered.

Elisabetta snapped, "That is not possible. Why would you speak such a lie?"

Serafino's gaze went suddenly cold as he met Elisabetta's challenge. "Read it again," he said. "The document bears the mark of his conviction. Lucianna is the child of their union. She has my mother's hair and eyes, she possesses my mother's brooch with my father's name scratched into the back, the one I saw my mother leave with her at the doorstep of the convent. And although I was only ten, I remember clearly the events of the night Giovanni was taken." He looked again at Lucianna and repeated, "My father is an honorable woolmonger." He gestured at the parchment. "What would you pay, dear one, to keep your father's identity a secret?"

"P-pay?" she stammered. A terrible shivering had seized her body. How could any of this be true?

"Your father is dead," Serafino said, his gaze boring into her now. "Our mother too, for which she may thank the mercy of heaven, for when my father sees you he will know at once who you are. She is beyond his punishment now, but you? When I tell him that I have discovered you in the house of Cosimo Gallo, do you think he will welcome you with open arms, the symbol of the shame and humiliation his wife brought upon him sixteen years ago with her betrayal of their bed?" Serafino shook his head. "No, dear one. I know the pride of Domenico Amorosi. He will hound you from the city." Serafino's gaze, clearly malicious now, slid to Elisabetta. "Do not think your father will escape the humiliation my father will heap upon him when he reveals that Cosimo Gallo has nourished a felon's by-blow in his home."

Elisabetta's embrace fell away. Lucianna wrapped her own arms around herself, trying to still her violent shaking.

Serafino's gaze returned to Lucianna. "Does Cosimo know what became of the pearl necklace that once graced his daughter's throat? When he learns of this" — he retrieved the parchment she had not realized she still clutched in her hand — "he most likely will believe you stole the necklace and sold it to make for yourself the little dowry that has won you the affection and offer of marriage from Vincenzo Mirolli. I think when I show this to Cosimo, dear one, my father may not be the only one wishing to hound you from the city."

"He has been watching you," Elisabetta hissed into Lucianna's ear. "He guessed all along who you were. He has been following us." Her dark eyes flashed at Serafino. "I sold the necklace," she declared. "But I can see that you have no shame in you not to lie." She paused, as if something in her own words had struck her. "How do we know it is not a lie, all of it? You are clearly despicable enough to invent such a tale merely to frighten us into giving you money."

"If this," he motioned at the court case, "and the brooch are not enough to convince you, then I know of one person who can confirm my words. At least, so I suspect. Before my mother died of her final illness, after she made her confession to the priest, she sent for the Abbess of Saint Catherine's to attend her. They were closeted away for a very long time and when the abbess came out, she looked grim even for a nun. What they spoke of I cannot say of a surety, but the timing of the visit suggested my mother desired to relieve herself of some guilt that still lay upon her conscience. I believe you knew the abbess as Mother Rosalba, dear one. She still presides over Saint Catherine's."

"But she never told me anything of my parentage," Lucianna protested. "I presumed she did not know."

"Or perhaps you simply never asked her."

It was true. Lucianna had assumed the nuns would have told her of her parents if they had known.

"So, shall we ask her now?" Serafino said. "I should be happy to escort you. If I am wrong, then you have nothing to fear and will never see me again."

Lucianna exchanged glances with Elisabetta, but they both knew returning to the convent was the only way. Only a denial by the abbess would protect Lucianna if Serafino took his lie to Elisabetta's father.

"Your parents did not give me leave to tell you of them, child."

So, then, Mother Rosalba *did* know the truth. *Lucianna knelt on the hard stones of the chapel of the Convent of Saint Catherine, her head meekly bowed before the aging abbess. Lucianna remembered when the wrinkles had been few in the Reverend Mother's face. Now they creased her skin like fine lines drawn in parchment. Lucianna held her hands laced at her breast as if in prayer, but she was certain the abbess could see how her fingers shook.*

"Please, Reverend Mother." *Her voice trembled, too.* "After all this time, I must know. Was Antonia Amorosi my mother?" *She inhaled a slightly shivering breath.* "And my father Domenico?"

Say yes. Oh please, say yes!

Mother Rosalba stood silent before her for a long moment, her hand clasped around the silver crucifix she always wore. Lucianna had grown soft since she had left the convent. She had forgotten how cold the stones seeped through her gown, how rough and unyielding the floor against her aching knees. She felt the small weight of the ruby brooch in the cuff of her sleeve where she had tied it, fearful that the abbess might chide her for vanity if saw Lucianna wearing it. From Mother Rosalba's stern face, Lucianna feared she did not intend to answer her questions.

"I would not ask you to betray her confidence if she still lived,"

Lucianna said. *"Nor would I ask if you were a priest — but you are not."* She saw the rebuke in the abbess's eye and quickly bowed her head. *"But if I ask amiss, then I beg your forgiveness."*

Her fingers began to grow numb she squeezed them so hard. They had always been cold to her, these nuns, colder than the stones she knelt upon. Why should she expect mercy from any of them now?

"I had hoped you would join us," the abbess spoke at last. *"We did our best to teach you humility, to prepare you for a life of obedience and meekness before God. But you remain as pert as ever. You are indeed like your mother."*

Lucianna's eyes darted up.

"Yes, you are the daughter of Antonia, but not of her husband, Domenico." The abbess frowned upon Lucianna with a familiar severity. *"Your mother was too lovely for her own good, and like you, she was haughty and proud and vain. But her sins came back to haunt her at the end. She told me of a handsome servant in her house named Giovanni. She disdained him as beneath her until her husband humiliated her with a serving girl. Then Antonia compounded his sin with her own by seducing Giovanni to spite him."*

Lucianna pressed the palms of her hands together and laid the edge of her forefingers against her lips. Mother Rosalba would think she prayed, but in truth, she did it to silence an impulse to scream a protest. Serafino spoke true. He spoke true!

Unaware of Serafino's role in Lucianna's visit to the convent, the abbess continued. *"But sin does not deal its consequences evenly upon men and women. Antonia found herself carrying Giovanni's child. Giovanni feared Domenico's wrath and fled, taking with him certain items from the household, by which he proved himself a thief at heart. He was caught by the city watch and punished. The timing of a journey by Domenico would make impossible any child Antonia carried his, and so together they agreed to send you to us at the convent. I never knew from whence you came until she summoned me before her death to unburden her soul to me."*

Lucianna lowered her hands very slowly. Pain and shame lashed through her, yet she found she still longed to know more of her unknown mother. *"Did — did she ask about me?"*

Another long, frowning pause. "Yes. But only if you were well. Then she sought for an assurance that you would remain in the convent and take the vows when you came of age. She feared lest her husband ever see your face outside the convent."

Lucianna gazed at the abbess, confused. "But you let me leave with Elisabetta."

"Cosimo Gallo was a very rich man who had paid us well to educate his daughter. We did not dare offend him and risk him refusing a final gift of his gratitude when he took his daughter home. Besides, Antonia was dead by then, and so was Giovanni. There was no one left for Domenico to punish should he ever see and know you."

Apparently she did not count any risk to Lucianna, perhaps because she trusted Cosimo Gallo's wealth to shield her. Or because she did not think me worth protecting if it cost the convent Cosimo's silver.

Then Serafino's threats rushed back in on her." I think when I show this to Cosimo, dear one, my father may not be the only one wishing to hound you from the city." *Serafino still had the court document, and if he sent Cosimo to Mother Rosalba as he had sent Lucianna —*

Lucianna started to her feet, ignoring her aching, trembling knees, and backed away from the woman who could destroy her future with a word.

"I must go." *The words came choking from Lucianna's throat.*

"Perhaps this at last will humble you," *Mother Rosalba called as Lucianna turned and ran from the chapel.* "Theft and wantonness run in your blood. It is not too late to return to us to spare shame to those in the world who have come to care for you."

Never. Never would she return to this hated place! Lucianna ran and ran until she sailed through the gates of the convent and landed in Elisabetta's arms. Mother Rosalba had refused to allow Elisabetta to join them in the chapel, but Elisabetta must have guessed that she had confirmed Serafino's story from the way Lucianna's shoulders shook with sobs.

She held Lucianna hard for a moment, then released her to whirl on Serafino who stood near them, grinning like a cat who had just swallowed a hapless sparrow.

"What will it take to make that" – Elisabetta nodded curtly towards the parchment – "go away and keep your tongue quiet?"

Before he could reply, Lucianna fumbled the ruby stone and its scrolling silver setting from the cuff of her sleeve where she had tied it. "Take this," she said. "I will never wear it again! Take it and sell it – "

Serafino sent a scornful glare down his nose at her, as though she had insulted him. "My father has kept the authorities of Venice searching for that for sixteen years. Do I look stupid enough to risk a sale of it being traced back to me? But you are a mere child, I cannot expect intelligence from you."

"But I have nothing else," Lucianna said, too distressed to be offended. "Except – except my dowry." If she gave him that, how would she explain its loss to Vincenzo? However much he loved her, his father would not let him marry her without a dowry.

"I should regret to accept that," Serafino said, though he did not look the least bit sorrowful. "But I had to give up my amethyst ring to bribe the official to lend me this" –he tapped the parchment – "so now I am afraid I have no money left to pay certain obligations I incurred over an awkward and unseemly incident I am too much a gentleman to soil your ears with."

Elisabetta gave a soft snort.

"And," he continued, "I have grown abysmally tired of these shabby clothes. My father is angry with me. He calls me spendthrift and refuses to give me another denaro. I ask no more than a loan, my dear one – "

Lucianna wavered. What else could she do?

Elisabetta's hand disappeared briefly beneath the draping sleeve of her silken gown. When it came out again, the diamond and sapphire bracelet she had donned that morning rested in her palm.

"If I give you this," she said to Serafino, "will you leave Venice and promise never to return?"

The covetous glitter in his eyes was all the answer Elisabetta appeared to need. She extended it towards Serafino, but a sudden, *vehement indignation jolted through Lucianna's confusion and fear. She seized Elisabetta's wrist, holding it short of Serafino's eager hand.*

"No! It is enough that you sold your necklace for me. I will not let you throw away your jewels on this rogue, this villain, this devil —"

"Harsh words for your brother, dear one," Serafino said with a laugh.

"No brother would treat me so," she spat at him. "If you take that you will be the thief!"

He reached out and scooped the bracelet from Elisabetta's hand. "My thanks," he said with a bow.

"Stop! I will report you to the guards —"

Elisabetta pressed her hand to Lucianna's mouth, muffling the rest of her outraged words.

"Stop," Elisabetta whispered. "Lucianna, stop."

Lucianna jerked the other girl's hand away, but her furious protest stumbled when she saw tears in Elisabetta's eyes.

"Don't you see?" Elisabetta said. "If my father learns of this, he will take you away from me. Lucianna, I could not bear it." She flung her arms around Lucianna and said with a small sob against her ear, "Sisters always. Always."

Lucianna hated the smirking triumph on Serafino's face as he bowed again and strolled away with the bracelet. She knew herself a coward to let him go, but Elisabetta's words chilled her. To lose the friend of her heart, to be cast out of the home she had so recently found, perhaps to be cast out of the city itself without a denaro to her name — She mentally struck the terrible vision away, even as she swore to herself that it was the last time, the very last time she would let Elisabetta sell a single jewel for her. They would not see Serafino again and he had taken the terrible truth of her birth with him.

"Always," Lucianna murmured back, hugging Elisabetta fiercely. She wiped away Elisabetta's tears, then she wiped away her own. "Let us go home and forget about this day."

Eight

Lucianna stared at Serafino and the wooden plate in his hands, heaped with roast venison in a sauce that smelled of onions, a chicken pasty and a pork tart, all topped with a kidney stew that was surely soaking the pasty and tart shells to mush.

"What are you doing?" she exclaimed as he swept past her into her bedchamber.

"Bringing you dinner. It became clear you spoke no idle threat yesterday when you failed to join us on the dais today. What sort of brother would I be if I let you starve?" He set the plate on a table near the bed, then turned and plucked a spoon and dining knife from his belt where he had tucked them.

He held the utensils out to her, but she ignored them. "I am not hungry. And if I were, looking on you would spoil my appetite. So take that mess away and yourself with it."

"Alas, I cannot. *Donna* Siri was upset by your absence, so I promised her I would bring you a few of your favorite dishes."

Lucianna crossed her arms, revolted by the mishmash he had made of the items on the dish. Serafino merely shrugged, sat down on the side of the bed with the plate in his lap, and tucked into the jumble of food himself.

"I spoke with your *amore* after you stormed from the hall yesterday," he said around a mouthful of tart so drenched in kidney stew that some of the broth dribbled down his chin. He wiped the broth away with his sleeve.

"I hope the gown I gave you to leave me in peace did not pay for that tunic," she said.

Serafino gave a brief, dismissive glance at the oily stain his mouth had left on his sleeve. "I confess, I was disappointed to learn that *Signor* Balduin is not as rich as that emerald ring and the silver needles he gave you had led me to hope. Still, he will be far from a pauper when *Don* Triston promotes him to castellan." Lucianna crossed to the bed to remove the nearest bolster before he could spill the increasingly swimming contents of the plate onto it." I do not doubt that we will all grow quite comfortable together at Dauvillier Castle and that *Signor* Balduin will be happy to lend me an occasional sum here and there as my needs require. He certainly will understand that his wife's brother cannot appear shabbily clothed before his friends."

She whirled at his words, inadvertently slamming the bolster into his shoulder.

"*You* are not coming to Dauvillier Castle with us! How can you think such a thing?"

"I am your brother —"

"My *half*-brother who never dared show his shameless face to anyone I knew in Venice, because they would have flung you out if you had, Walter, Simon, Alessandro, even Siri!"

Serafino shoveled another spoonful into his mouth. "You should not have told Siri about my gambling," he said, rolling an admonishing eye at his sister as he chomped on the food.

Lucianna felt a small chill steal down her back. "How do you know what I might have said to Siri?"

"The boy blabbed it, *Don* Triston's son. I met him in the garden. He said Siri wanted him to stay out of my way. Now I know why she is so cold when I sit next to her at dinner."

"It is all I told her, I swear."

"*Si*, because you fear she would fling *you* out along with me if she knew all of the truth. Or that *Don* Triston would. Siri might try to defend you, but do you imagine *Don* Triston would trust you anywhere near his wife once he learned all you purloined from her first husband?"

"I stole nothing! I never gave you anything she had not freely given to me." Yet even as Lucianna said it, her conscience seared. They may have been gifts, but it had felt like theft for she had known Siri's love and generosity would replace whatever items Lucianna had "lost."

"I suspect *Don* Alessandro would have thought differently had he known where your gowns, jewels and trinkets went."

"To you," Lucianna said bitterly. "Because of the horrible things you threatened."

Serafino's lip curled into that sneer that lay so thinly concealed beneath the virtuous smiles with which he beguiled the unwary. "And if I choose to say that you conspired with me to seduce *Donna* Siri into giving you so many beautiful things that you and I might share in their profit? And that you have not changed your fraudulent colors, whatever *Donna* Siri might wish to think, but hoped to embezzle afresh from her new inheritance? *Si*, she might doubt me, but what of *Don* Triston and *Signor* Balduin when they learn that you are the daughter of a thief?"

Lucianna clutched the bolster so tightly to her breast it was a wonder the seams did not burst. "You dare not say that." She thrust up her chin defiantly, even though she knew it was useless to challenge him.

"I dared before, *cara*. I told the truth to Vincenzo."

Into his mouth went another spoonful of slop. This time he waited until he gulped it down before he spoke again.

"This is not Venice, *cara*. I could not pretend there, for too many knew me as the shiftless, carousing, womanizing son of a woolmonger. But at least I was a legitimate son of a woolmonger, not the base born daughter of his faithless wife and the servant she seduced, who fled in fear when he got her with child, taking with him a brace of candlesticks, a silver goblet, and our mother's ruby brooch—the one *la forsa* never found among his things because our mother hid it in the blanket she wrapped you in before she laid you on the doorstep of the sisters of the *conventa di Santa Caterina*."

And abandoned me, a nameless foundling. Mother Rosalba, the abbess, had christened her Lucianna for she had been discovered on the howling cold morn of Saint Lucia's Day. All her dreams shattered in an instant fifteen years later on that bitter day on the Piazza San Marco, none more so than the precious figment of the golden young man who had come to her in a dream and made her feel safe and loved on the loneliest night of her life in the convent.

Elisabetta's bracelet had not kept Serafino away. Rather than winning his permanent silence, he had made them pay again and again to keep secret Lucianna's shameful origins. The one time Lucianna had put her foot down and said *non più*, he had shown his black soul by carrying out the threat he always made when they hinted of defiance. He had told Vincenzo Mirolli a week before his wedding to Lucianna. Vincenzo had agreed not to spread the tale, but Lucianna had never forgotten the repugnance that replaced his formerly fond gazes at her and the anguished crack of her heart when she had run after him to stay him from leaving her and he had snarled, "Do not touch me."

Elisabetta had held her, weeping out her shattered heart in Vincenzo's wake, mingling her tears with Lucianna's and murmuring over and over, "You will find love again, you will. I know it with everything that is in me."

But Lucianna had spurned every other offer for her hand, winning herself a reputation for pride and haughtiness among the merchants' sons. What else could she have done? She knew how quickly and gleefully Serafino could and would destroy her life if she ever sought to defy him again. Humiliating enough to let Elisabetta pay him with silver and jewels when Lucianna failed to sell enough of her embroidery to satisfy him. She could not let him despoil a husband, too.

She should never have relaxed the wall she had thrust up around her heart, but how could she have guessed that Serafino would find her in far off Poitou? She had panicked and had succumbed afresh to his blackmail when he had appeared in the market town. But she had realized quickly that she had not loved Vincenzo one tenth as much as she loved Sir Balduin—too much to endure Sir Balduin learning the truth and too much to lie. Leaving was the only way.

"*Non più.*" Lucianna repeated the words she had spoken to Serafino twenty-nine years ago. She felt her voice strengthen with her determination. "No more. If you tell *Signor* Balduin or *Don* Triston or anyone, it will benefit you nothing, for nothing you or *Signor* Balduin can do will persuade me to stay here and marry him, and if I do not stay you cannot force me to steal anymore for you."

"But that is the beauty of it all," Serafino said. "You shall not have to steal for me. *Signor* Balduin will 'loan' me all I need, because I am your devoted brother and he wishes to see you happy. Serafino Amorosi, the woolmonger's shiftless son, is a forgotten man in Venice. Here I am Serafino Fabio. We shall be full-blood siblings, you and I, our parents as respectable as you and Elisabetta invented them all those years ago, my only vice being a slight addiction to the dice—"

"—and drinking too much and being too fond of women you are not married to," Lucianna said. "Men and women our age do not easily change, Serafino, and a man like you never changes at all. *Signor* Balduin will grow weary of you, and then he will grow weary of me. *No.* I have ended it between us. I will not marry him, and nothing you can do or say will make me."

Serfino dragged the spoon across the wooden plate, scraping up the remains of the food his wolfish appetite had mostly devoured. "I do not say it will be easy to win him back," he said as though Lucianna had not spoken. "Not after you called him a buffoon."

She gasped. She had called Sir Balduin many things in an attempt to drive a wedge between them, but she had never called him that! "Did he say I called him a buffoon?"

"It is what he is convinced you think him," Serafino said vaguely. "Not that he does not deserve the epithet after that appalling song of his. I cannot blame you for being mortified. It made my ears ache merely to listen to him."

Lucianna bristled. "His voice was very handsome before he grew befuddled at the end."

She had seen the consternation in Sir Balduin's eyes as he had veered off course a tune that had both surprised and delighted her for the clarity of a baritone she had never guessed he possessed. How could she not feel herself flattered that he would risk the privacy she knew he held so dear to court her in so public and melodious a way, even if he had stumbled a bit with the descriptions of her hair and eyes? It had not been offense at the fumbling he had fallen into that had made her spring from her chair and accuse him of drunkenness. It had been the almost overpowering melting of her own resolve and her terror that Serafino might sense it. Still, she had not been able to leave Sir Balduin without attempting to smooth the hurt she knew she had heaped on him once again. Even as she had rejected him afresh, she had spoken of his courage and praised his song and kisses. His kisses. She felt herself quiver at the memories. How could he ever think she could call him a buffoon?

Lucianna saw Serafino watching her, a quirk of amusement on his mouth. She had let her thoughts drift dangerously and Serafino had observed it.

"You still want him, *cara*."

"What I want is to go home to Venice, and there is no way for you to stop me."

Serafino set the plate on the table beside the bed and licked off the gravy that had dripped over the edges onto his fingers. "Perhaps not. But how is it you will go? As the proud and dignified Lucianna Fabio? Or as Lucianna, the thief's by-blow, who proved herself her father's daughter by absconding with this when she fled?"

He dug a thumb into a pouch attached to his belt, and drew out a silver chain on which dangled Sir Balduin's emerald ring.

She gasped. "How do you have that? I gave it back to *Signor* Balduin!"

"Flung it at him, as I recall," Serafino said, swinging the ring on the chain. "Your stoic Frenchman is quite the romantic, *cara*. He put it on this chain and wore it inside his tunic, no doubt to keep your remembrance close to his heart. I comforted him as he sat in the garden yesterday. I told him I was certain I could thaw you towards him and we embraced, as future brothers-in-law. I believe my familiarity startled him, which allowed me to undo the clasp and slip this from his neck while I held him fast against my breast. I'd thought merely to pocket the silver chain to pay off a wager I lost in a tavern in that dreary market town where I met you before my dicing companions traced me here, but I found this lovely thing attached." He flicked the ring with a finger so that it twirled the chain to the left, then respun to the right. "I will settle for this if I must. I told you I could likely pay off my debts with this for a year."

"*Ladro!*" Lucianna made a grab for the ring, but he whisked it out of her reach. "Thief! Give it to me!"

His eyes gleamed with a familiar unholy mischief, but it still startled her when he suddenly dropped the chain and ring into her hand.

"As you wish, *cara*. But how will you explain to your *amore* that it is in your possession again?"

Lucianna stared down at the deep green jewel with a slowly dawning horror. She could not accuse Serafino of stealing it when it lay in Lucianna's own palm. Serafino would deny it, and point the finger at her sordid parentage.

Lucianna did not fear losing Siri's love. She had helped Elisabetta raise her from a babe and she trusted Siri to understand the conflict Serafino had bound her in for so many years. But Triston was unlikely to be so forbearing, even for Siri's sake, and Sir Balduin— The vision of him staring at Lucianna with revulsion, as Vincenzo had, dropped her down, weak with horror, on the bed beside her villainous half-brother.

Serafino patted her cold cheek as though he were the most loving of siblings. "There, there, *cara*. All you have to do is marry him, and that, from the way you gazed at him while he sang to you, you will hardly find unpleasant. As soon as the wedding is over, I will help you plant the ring in some corner of his chamber where he can find it with a broken clasp, right where it 'fell off' without him noticing. We shall live very merrily together, the three of us, you will see."

He rose, picked up the plate, and left her, no doubt to reassure Siri with the vanished meal that however dismal Lucianna's spirits, her appetite remained perfectly healthy.

Lucianna gazed after him for several long, conflicted moments, hating herself for the elated little corner of her heart that welcomed a trap that would make her Sir Balduin's wife. But she could not let herself give into the temptation. Everything she had said to Serafino was true. She could not live happily watching him bleed away Sir Balduin's modest wealth, knowing Sir Balduin tolerated and indulged Serafino's vices for love of her. The long, steady drip of Serafino's poison would slowly but surely wear away Sir Balduin's patience, and eventually, his affection for Lucianna. However blissful marriage might be in the beginning, the joyful years, whether long or short, could not be worth the bitter ending she knew must irrevocably come.

And always would hover the oppressive fear that if ever she sought to cross him, Serafino would tell Sir Balduin the truth of her birth. Sir Balduin would not merely grow tired of her then. He would hate her for having deceived him.

A teardrop splashed on the deep green stone winking up at her from her palm. Once a token of love, it now mocked her cowardice. For she knew there was one way to frustrate Serafino's smug scheme, yet she shrank from it like a frightened, fluttering sparrow. She, Lucianna, who had always been called tigress, fury, spitfire, even once by an overawed suitor in her youth, an Amazon for her bold, fiery ways, had in truth been a pathetic, selfish, frightened child to have allowed Serafino to manipulate her so shamefully for nearly thirty years.

"Men and women our age do not easily change," she had told Serafino. But if she truly loved Sir Balduin, she knew she must do just that. She must choke down her fear and embrace her shame and tell Sir Balduin the truth herself.

Her heart hammered so hard she thought she would be ill as she rose from the bed and stepped towards the door. She paused to try to still it, then lifted the ring to her lips, thinking the love it had once betokened might somehow give her courage. The silver chain slid dangling through her fingers and her eye lit upon its clasp.

The thought flowed into her mind before she could stop it. Serafino himself had given her another possible escape. There was no need to wait until after a wedding to place the ring where Sir Balduin would find it. Lucianna could do it now, herself, some place where it could bear no possible connection to her or Serafino.

She struggled desperately with herself, the woman who longed for the relief of honesty against the child who wanted to be remembered with love when she was gone. The child won, as always.

Nine

How could he have lost it? He had kept the chain tucked in his clothing since the day she had hurled the ring back into his hands, yet chain and ring had both undeniably vanished. At first, Sir Balduin assumed the clasp must have broken during a change of clothing, but he had spent the entire night searching his bedchamber. Ransacking it had been more like it, for as his alarm at its disappearance increased, he had upended every object in the chamber, great and small, and even crawled under the bed when dawn had allowed enough grey light through the window for him to see murkily beneath it. He had discovered a missing shoe, a bent spoon, a bronze brooch he'd misplaced more than a month ago, three copper coins, a broken chess piece he'd meant to mend, and a great deal of lint that made him sneeze. But there had been no sign of his grandmother's ring.

Bad enough that he had lost the only heirloom handed down to him from his family, but Lucianna had worn it long enough upon her finger for him to forget about his grandmother and think entirely of the woman he had grown to love and hoped to marry when he gazed on it. It would always say *Lucianna* to him now. He had intended to cherish it as though her very memory dwelt in the fiery green depths that glowed like her eyes when she kissed him. Without it, what would he have to remember her by when she had gone?

Having come up fruitless in his chamber, he had spent the day retracing his steps from yesterday. He had passed the morning searching the hall where he had made that humiliating spectacle of himself, even while the servants came in to set the table afresh for another dinner. He hunted so long he had no time to change his lint covered clothes before the rest of the castle came in to dine. Except for Lucianna and her brother. She had kept her vow not to attend, so he had known Serafino had failed to convince her to forgive him. Sir Balduin sat through a miserable meal without her, too occupied with mentally flailing himself for yesterday's stupidity to care for the snickers and smirks that still occasionally broke from those household members who had witnessed the debacle.

Sir Balduin had questioned every servant he could find, including each one who brought a platter of food onto the dais, but none of them had seen the chain or ring. As soon as the meal was over he headed for the garden. He did not know how he could have lost it there during his exchange with Serafino, but it had fallen off sometime between yestermorn and yesternight, and Sir Balduin would leave no stone or rosebush unturned in his determined hunt.

Once again when he reached the garden, he found Perrin there before him. This time the boy sat cross-legged in the flowery mead, with a wax tablet in his lap and a stylus in his hand. An autumn wind tossed his black curls about his face so that he had to push the hair out of his eyes as he looked up at Sir Balduin's footstep.

"Father Michel said I could practice tracing my Latin lines out here today," the boy said quickly, as though to preempt another scolding.

Sir Balduin waved a distracted hand. "Have you seen my emerald ring?"

"The one you gave to Lady Lucianna?"

"Aye. The chain broke yesterday. I thought it might have done so while I was here with her brother."

Sir Balduin walked around the edges of the garden while Perrin laid his tablet aside and scampered through the mead on his hands and knees, searching through the low growing flowers. Sir Baldin bent over to lift the lower branches of the rose bush Perrin had beheaded the previous day, then winced and bit off a gasp as his knees popped and the muscles of his back protested, reminding him that a man his age had had no business to be scrambling around underneath beds, no matter how urgent the quest.

"Shall I look there for you?" Perrin asked.

Sir Balduin flushed slightly. It made him feel an old man to nod, but he feared if he dropped to his knees again, he might never regain his feet. It disgusted him how stiff his muscles had become since the injury to his hip had impeded his ability to train as regularly as he once had done.

Perrin dove under the rose bush. "Are you going to give it back to Lady Lucianna if you find it?" his voice floated from beneath the leaves.

Sir Balduin dropped gloomily down on the wattle wall. "She has made it clear she has no use for it or me." He cursed the gruffness of his voice when Perrin peeked out at him, then disappeared under the bush again.

"I heard Siri tell Papa that she cried so hard for you it frightened her. I mean Lady Lucianna cried, not Siri. Siri likes you very much, but I do not think she would cry over you. Did you do something to break Lady Lucianna's heart?"

"I mangled her Italian and offended her with a gift and made a fool of myself and her at dinner." Sir Balduin sighed. "And apparently I am also inconsiderate and refuse to confide in her. And she thinks I called her fat."

"Here it is!"

Despite his aching muscles, Sir Balduin leapt up from the wall.

"Oh, bah. It is just a rock." A stone roughly the size of the ring but otherwise bearing no resemblance to an emerald came spinning out from beneath the bush. A moment later, Perrin

112

came out, too. "It's not under there." He sat down and wrapped his arms around his knees. "Did you really call Lady Lucianna fat? She's not nearly as fat as Siri is now."

"Lady Siri is expecting a baby," Sir Balduin said.

"Oh, I know. I'm to have a brother or sister. Papa says it will do me good, though I can't see how it will." Perrin shrugged. "One day Papa suggested that Siri was eating too many sweets and Siri burst into tears and said, 'I am not fat, I am having a baby,' and Papa said, 'That is not what I meant—', but I never found out what he *did* mean because he just started apologizing until Siri quit crying, and then she apologized too, and then they looked at each other all goggly-eyed—you know, the way you and Lady Lucianna used to look at each other—and the next thing I knew they were kissing, so I left the room."

Perrin fixed a gaze on Sir Balduin that was almost unnerving for its directness. "I thought it was all very silly, but I learned that women don't like to be called fat, so maybe you should apologize to Lady Lucianna and kiss her." He spoiled this sage advice by slightly wrinkling his nose.

"I have apologized," Sir Balduin muttered, sitting back down. Well, not for the song. Lucianna had not given him a chance, and he did not suppose there was an apology large enough for that fiasco anyway.

"And she did not forgive you?" Perrin asked. "Maybe it only works with a kiss. Bah," he repeated, causing Sir Balduin to wonder where the boy had picked up the exclamation. Perrin's nose wrinkled again. "Women seem to like it. Kissing, I mean. I say bah and bah!"

"You are beginning to sound like a sheep," Sir Balduin said.

Perrin's vivid blue eyes danced wickedly. "I heard Gille the goose girl say it. Father Michel said it is not refined for a baron's son, but he won't let me swear, either. I have to say something when I am vexed. So I say bah."

"And kissing vexes you?"

"I don't understand it. Papa says I will when I am older, but . . ."

"But 'bah?'" Sir Balduin inquired, amused in spite of himself as the boy trailed off.

Perrin nodded. "You are old, though, and so is Lady Lucianna, so you probably understand already. Why don't you kiss her and apologize again? It worked for Papa and Siri."

"Some things cannot be solved with a kiss, Perrin." Or could they? It could not possibly be that simple. Sir Balduin's heart jolted slightly. Could it?

Perrin crawled over to his tablet and set it in his lap again. "Well, I think maybe she wants to make up, because I saw her letting herself into your chamber when I came out from my lessons with Father Michel."

"You what?" Sir Balduin spoke so sharply that Perrin jumped. He quickly moderated his tone. "The chapel is nowhere near my chamber. You could not have seen any such thing."

"I did," the boy insisted. "I met Lord Serafino at the head of the stairs—I suppose he must be a lord if Lady Lucianna is a lady. He was grinning and chuckling, and he tousled my hair when he saw me, which I did not like for he held a greasy looking plate in his hands. He asked me if I knew where you were. I said you must be at dinner, but that it was probably near its ending. Then he sent a long look over his shoulder at the passageway behind him, the one that goes east, before he chuckled again and went on down the stairs."

Perrin picked up the stylus and began writing in the wax as he continued.

"I wondered why he stared so long that way, so when he was gone, I went to peer around the corner. I saw Lady Lucianna. I thought she looked sad. I was worried that she had been crying again and I knew that would make Siri unhappy, so I decided to try to think of something to cheer her up and I followed her. But then she let herself into your chamber. I thought maybe you were in there and she was going to make up with you and then Siri would be happy again, so I came out here to leave you alone. But you really

114

were at dinner instead." He glanced up to catch Sir Balduin's surprise. "You have gravy on your tunic."

Sir Balduin brushed at the stain, thankful it had dried too much to smear. He plucked off a piece of lint that clung to his breast alongside it.

Perrin held up the tablet to Sir Balduin. "Does that look right?"

"A-U-D-I-E-N-S—" Sir Balduin recited the letters, then sounded them out. "Ah-oo-dee-ehns . . . Bah, lad, how should I know? I do not read Latin. What is it supposed to say?"

"*Audiens, sapiens sapientior erit.*" The strange words rolled effortlessly off the boy's tongue, bearing no resemblance to Sir Balduin's attempted pronunciation. "'By listening, the wise will become wiser.' Or something like that. Father Michel says it comes from the Bible. I think he made me write it because I said learning grammar was dull."

"Has Lady Siri taught you any Italian?" Sir Balduin asked, curious.

"Oh, *si*. It is not that different from French, really. 'Listen' is *ascolatare*—well, I suppose that is different from how we say it. But 'wise' is nearly the same. Look." He rubbed out his Latin lines and wrote *saggio* next to the French *sage*."

It seemed simple when Sir Balduin saw the words side by side like that. "But they are not all so easy," he protested. "You admitted that 'listen' is different."

"That's true." Perrin wrote *ascolatare* next to the familiar *écouter*. "Is that why you called Lady Lucianna fat? Because you mixed it up with something else? Siri hasn't taught me how to say fat yet."

Sir Balduin grunted. He wished heartily that Lucianna had never tried to teach him a single Italian syllable.

Then he remembered what they had been discussing before Perrin had distracted him with Latin. "You are certain you saw her near my chamber?"

"I saw her open the door and go in." Sir Balduin was fairly certain the boy was not supposed to use his sleeve to rub out the Italian and French he had scratched into the wax.

Perrin had surely been mistaken. Lucianna clung far too fast to propriety to enter a man's chambers. Heaven knew she had guarded Siri with the ferociousness of a lioness her cub when they had first come to Vere—although Sir Balduin knew his own attempts to woo Lucianna had allowed Siri to elude her companion's stern eye sufficiently often for her to win Triston's heart. Sir Balduin still treasured a particularly satisfying memory of a moonlit night in this garden where he had drawn Lucianna after a banquet Siri had held for their neighbors, an enchanted night that had melted Lucianna unexpectedly into his arms for the first time and warmed her lips like luscious honey beneath his mouth.

He glanced up at the clouds, wondering how long it had been since Perrin saw Lucianna at his door. A pity Sir Balduin had not known. He might have intercepted her. Now it was too late. Or was it? He slapped his hands against his knees. She had come to his door for a reason. Even if it had been an ominous one, to rebuke him for his lamentable song yesterday, he would have rejoiced just to gaze into her lovely, wrathful face. And if there had been some slim, unlikely chance that she had come to "make up with him," as Perrin had speculated— Oh, that would be impossible. And yet the infinitesimal hope launched Sir Balduin again to his feet.

Perrin looked up. "Are you going to find her?"

Sir Balduin nodded. "Thank you, Perrin. Dinner has been over for some time now, so don't linger in the garden much longer. Father Michel will be expecting you back at your lessons."

"Bah," the boy said, but added, "very well."

Sir Balduin strode to the garden's gate, but as he swung it open, Perrin's voice sailed after him, "Don't forget to kiss her!"

Sir Balduin met Siri and Serafino at the foot of the stairs.

Serafino appeared to be trying to charm her with one of his angelic smiles and some words that flowed from his lips in those same enchanting accents that Lucianna spoke in, an accent that disappeared in Siri's voice when she spoke French. The Italian lilt in Serafino's voice made Sir Balduin's heart trip excitedly for the encounter he prayed lay ahead for him. Siri was listening to Serafino with a tapping toe that hinted of impatience which she only checked when Sir Balduin paused to briefly greet them.

Sir Balduin excused his failure to linger. "Forgive me, but I soiled my tunic at dinner. I am off to change."

"But *signore*," Serafino protested, "I was hoping to speak to you of my sister—"

"Later," Sir Balduin called over his shoulder. If luck was with him, perhaps he could heal his breach with Lucianna without Serafino's aid.

He tried to reign in his excitement as he swept on up the stairs. He ought not to allow his hopes to soar. But while Lucianna might rebuke him roundly to his face at the moment of an offense, she was not a vindictive wench, as he had observed some poor husbands possessed in their wives. Upon reflection, Sir Balduin knew she would not have come seeking him in his own chamber merely to rub salt into his wounds. Something else had brought her there. Even if it had only been a desire to cry truce, that would indicate a degree of softening that perhaps—just perhaps he could reignite into something more promising.

He heard Siri's voice chime rather sharply behind him and wondered what Serafino might have said to provoke her, but Sir Balduin was too eager in his quest to pay any heed to the words of their exchange. He paused only for an instant at the head of the stairs, casting a longing glance down the west-leading passageway that led to Lucianna's chambers. He could not seek her out with a gravy stain and lint clinging to his tunic. He would change it for the blue surcote that she had once remarked brought out a hint of that shade in his grey eyes. And that girdle she had embroidered for him with the golden acorns, the symbol of his house which he had long ago abandoned in service to Triston's family—he would wear that, too. The symbol had suddenly become dear to him again on the day he had asked Lucianna to be his wife. He vividly recalled how, as he had let out his anxiously suspended breath at her blushing assent, the obscure future he had grown to envision for himself suddenly took on vibrant meaning at his anticipation of sharing his life with her. He had intended to ask her to embroider a pair of twin girdles, interweaving the acorn with the symbol of her Fabio house, the grapevine, for them to wear together upon their wedding day.

The acorn—strength, independence and antiquity. The grapevine—strength and lasting friendship. *Lasting love.* At their age, that should have been easy to achieve. But instead, they had quarreled—no, he would not say foolishly. That would be to disrespect her feelings, as baffling as most of her complaints remained to him. But he supposed if women were not so utterly bewildering, he would not have found Lucianna so wonderfully intriguing.

Sir Balduin reached his door and pushed it open. He froze for a moment on viewing the disarray he had left his chamber in. He had tumbled his clothes out of their chests, lest his ring had somehow fallen inside one of them. Garments lay everywhere, strewn across the floor, tossed across the bed. He had scattered his shoes and boots, his belts and girdles, what little other jewelry he owned, mostly items of brass, a few of glass, some of brightly colored wooden beads. The broken chess piece lay just inside the threshold where he had flung it from beneath the bed in frustration. He groaned silently. Had his blue surcote, wherever it was, lain long enough in a heap to set creases in the cloth beyond the power of his hand to smooth out? What if it were covered with piles of lint he had dragged out from under the bed with him? Lucianna admired cleanliness and neatness, two virtues he had spent a great deal of time cultivating since the day she had arrived at Vere Castle.

Then a movement caught the corner of his eye at the same instant a small gasp struck his ear. He turned his head and met an emerald gaze more lustrous than any jewel he might have misplaced. Lucianna? In his chamber? What was she doing here?

The question blinked out as he realized he did not give two snaps for the answer. She had come looking for him and he was not about to let her leave before he had made it blazingly clear to her what she meant to him. Perrin's words rang in his ears and drove him across the floor, heedless of the tunics and hose and surcotes his feet crushed to reach her. He pulled away the hand that had flown over her mouth, dragged her into his arms, and kissed her.

Lucianna slid her arms around Sir Balduin's neck just in time to prevent her knees from succumbing to the pleasure that threatened to buckle them. How long had it been since she had allowed him to kiss her? Weeks only, yet it had begun to seem like a distant imagining that he had ever held her thus. This was why she had fought so hard to evade him, fear that her body would betray her in his embrace, just as she felt it doing now. The urgent twining of her arms, her ardent return of his kiss, the way her heart thudded so fervently he must surely feel its driving beat against his breast — she knew she must stop herself somehow, but all her traitorous soul did was melt her deeper into the flame of his love.

She resisted a moment when his hands moved to her cheeks. If he broke the kiss, he would break the spell that she wanted to lose herself in forever. Reality would rush back in. What would she say, how would she explain her presence here? Perhaps she could yet drop the ring where he would later find it, spurn him afresh, and fly from the room and Vere Castle and Poitou. But all her determination flowed away like water in his caress. It did not buttress her resolve to see the exultant curve of his lips as they pulled away from hers.

"Lucianna! I thought I had lost you forever with that clumsy song of mine, but that was no kiss of farewell you just dealt me. That you should come seeking me thus, that you should forgive me — Oh, my angel!"

Her lungs constricted painfully. How could she find the will to do what she must do when he gazed at her with so much adoration in his eyes? She struggled to find breath to check him, to strike away his illusions, no matter how she shrank from shattering that glow, but a voice rapped first from the doorway.

"Your angel. *My* sister. I am shocked, *signore*, truly. I presumed you a man of honor, but I see that I mistook your character."

Lucianna tore her face from Sir Balduin's cupping hands and stared in horror at Serafino standing on the threshold. It took a moment through her dismay to realize he was not alone. Siri's diminutive frame stood at his side.

Siri jerked at Serafino's sleeve. "Come away. They are not children. Let them be."

"I am afraid I cannot oblige you, *signora*. My sister may be, shall we say, a little beyond the bloom of youth, but she is still a maiden whose virtue I consider myself honor bound to defend."

Lucianna saw Sir Balduin's face redden even as she felt her own blood drain from her cheeks.

"This is not what it appears, sir," Sir Balduin said stiffly. "I did not lure your sister to my chamber. I had no notion I would find her here. Why, you saw me yourself come from below stairs. I passed you and Lady Siri on the steps —"

"*Si*, quite cheerfully, if I recall, and in such a hurry that you scarce paused to say *buongiorno*. Which only makes your knavery more audacious, knowing you were on your way to rendezvous with my sister right under my very nose."

Despite his words, Lucianna observed that Serafino looked more smug than outraged. Sir Balduin fell into a spluttering defense, but before he could organize it into any coherence, Serafino added, "There is, of course, only one way to make this right. I trust I need not speak more plainly, *signore*?"

Sir Balduin's grey brows plunged down at the implied

ultimatum. "You have completely mistaken matters, sir. I would never insult your sister's virtue. But if you mean you expect me to marry her, then you may put your mind to rest. That has been the greatest desire of my heart for many months. Now that she has forgiven me—"

Sir Balduin reached for her nearest hand, the one she still had balled into a fist. She flung it behind her back in a panic. "I have not forgiven you. How can you think I would ever forgive the way you humiliated me in the hall?"

He turned his head to gaze at her in bewilderment. "But the way you kissed me just now." He lowered his voice. "You kissed me like that the day I asked you to marry me. The day you said you loved me."

Despite the murmured words, she felt Serafino's gaze fixed upon them and knew how he strained to hear. How could she lie when Sir Balduin had tasted the truth in her lips?

Si, I love you," she said, tears starting to her eyes, "but it changes nothing. I cannot marry a man so insensitive, so selfish, so—so oafish." Nothing but cruelty could drive the wedge irrevocably between them. She gestured at the clothing strewn about. "And see! He is a sloven as well, I will forever be picking up after him." In truth, the disorder of his chamber *had* dismayed her. "*No.* I cannot bind my life to a man who will only make me miserable. Nothing has changed. As soon as *Donna* Siri's *bambino* is born, I—"

"But I'm afraid things *have* changed, *cara*," Serafino interrupted. "I really cannot overlook the fact that I stumbled upon you and *Signor* Balduin intimately entwined in the middle of his chamber. Or—" he paused "—perhaps it is not *Signor* Balduin's character I misjudged, but your own, and perhaps this is not the first time you have been—er—thus entwined here. Can it be that my maiden sister is no longer a maiden?" Serafino feigned shock at the thought, but rushed on over Lucianna's angry denial and Sir Balduin's heated defense of her. "The Fabio name is a proud one, and I cannot have it sullied. I am still your brother and responsible for your reputation. The two of you must marry, and that in all haste, before word of this day flies all over the castle."

Lucianna saw Siri's eyes grow wide, as though the possibility that Lucianna and Sir Balduin might already be lovers had never occurred to her.

Lucianna felt her previously cold face grow fiery with indignation at Serafino's slur. "We are not—"

But Serafino flung up a hand and again spoke over her words. "Stay, *cara*. You are right to rebuke me. As *Donna* Siri says, you are not a child and how you choose at your age to live your life should, perhaps, be no concern of mine. If only you had been more circumspect I might have agreed, however reluctantly, to look the other way. But the damage has been done and there is no rectifying it now. Marriage is the only way to remedy this reckless indiscretion. It really is no use," he added, cutting off her renewed protest, "to try to persuade me of your innocence. What other reason could you have for being in *Signor* Balduin's chamber?"

Serafino's gaze flicked for the barest instant to her fisted hand before returning to her face. He knew. He knew she held the ring concealed in her palm, and worse, that she had come here to hide it where Sir Balduin would find it. Had this always been Serafino's plan, to plant the idea in her mind, then maneuver Sir Balduin to find her here? No wonder Serafino had "conveniently" come upon their embrace. He looked so self-satisfied she wanted to hit him.

She hissed, "Think what you like. Shout my 'shame' from the rooftops. I will not marry *Signor* Balduin."

Serafino crossed the floor and touched her balled hand. "No?"

She raised her chin. "*No.*"

Sir Balduin cleared his throat rather loudly, as if to force their attention back to him. "I believe I have some say in this matter, sir," he said to Serafino with a vehemence that startled Lucianna. "Nothing could bring me more happiness than to marry your sister, but to force upon her a union against her will, compelled by a false accusation? I am not such a villain as to agree to that. Your sister's virtue remains unstained and I will not disgrace her before the world by allowing your vile suspicions to drive us to the altar. She will marry me for love and of her own volition, with the honor that is due her, or we shall part as she says she wishes." He looked at Lucianna, misery flowing in alongside the kindling in his eyes and whispered, "Even if it breaks my heart."

Serafino said drily, "Your sentiments are laudable, *signore,* more than my sister's behavior deserves, for if she did not come to your chamber to seduce you, I can think of no other reason for her presence here."

Lucianna tore her gaze away from Sir Balduin's hurt, gliding past Siri's concerned eyes, to meet Serafino's challenge. From the glint in his eyes she knew he was determined to coerce her, but nothing he could do or say would make her yield to his desire.

When she confronted him with several moments of resistant silence, he blinked away the glint and shammed his face into a slowly dawning misgiving. "Unless . . ."

She struggled to squelch the quivering in her belly. He trailed off, giving her a chance to stop him. *Nothing will make me yield.*

His gaze, wide with chagrin, fell to her fist. "*Cara,* tell me you have not succumbed to your old temptations?"

Nothing. Not even this.

Serafino turned towards Sir Balduin, as she had known he would at her silence, and uttered in tones shot through with consternation, "*Signore,* forgive me, but if what I suspect is true, *veramente,* I have maligned you. *Cara.*" He stretched out his hand to Lucianna. What are you concealing in your grasp?"

That lift of his auburn brows appeared a stern query to the others in the room, but to her it was a grim threat that she had crumbled before too many times before. She knew exactly what he would say next if she did not crumble again. Every word still stung clear as shards of broken glass in her heart.

They had driven Vincenzo from her in the spring of her life. They would drive Sir Balduin away now in her autumn, leaving her a cold, bleak, empty winter of a future.

I will lose him either way. Better one swift, searing break than to watch the long, slow withering of his love.

She braced herself for the storm about to burst over her, opened her fist, and held out the ring on its chain.

Relief flooded Sir Balduin's face. "I have searched for that high and low today, this bedroom, the hall, even the garden. Lucianna, where did you find it?"

She longed to seize upon the lie he offered her, but Serafino said in nearly the same instant, shaking his head in condemnation, "Ah, *cara*! What else have you pilfered from your beloved?" to which she blurted out indignantly, "Nothing!" before she realized how the word sealed her guilt.

Serafino heaved a great sigh. "I had hoped—nay, I had prayed that you had changed. *Signore*," he said to Sir Balduin, "my apologies. I cannot tell you how awkward this is, how mortifying to confess myself mistaken, for as distressing as my first suspicions would have been had they been true, this, I fear, is far worse. My sister, I regret, has a long habit of— *ahimè*! I know no way to put this delicately. The embarrassing fact is that my sister has a long habit of taking things that do not belong to her."

Sir Balduin's gaze grew more puzzled as he studied the object in Lucianna's palm. The question Serafino sought to plant clearly drifted into Sir Balduin's head, though to her gratitude, she watched his struggle to dismiss it.

"That is absurd. She must have found it somewhere and come to return it to me."

But even as he said it, his mouth turned down in a frown. Why had she not brought it to him somewhere in the open? The hall, the garden, or stood knocking on his chamber door rather than slipping surreptitiously into his chamber? She knew she guessed his thoughts aright when he lifted his gaze back to her face.

"Lucianna," he said softly, "I do not understand."

"*Signore,*" Serafino said, "it pains me to tell you of this, but my sister is not what you think her." The sweep of his eyes encompassed Siri now. "She is not what any of you have thought her. Everything about her, even her name, is a lie."

Siri stepped to Lucianna's side and glared at Serafino with an anger so bright, Lucianna thought for a moment she was staring again at Elisabetta.

"I will not listen to any more of this. You may think to deceive Sir Balduin with these slanders, but I have known Lucianna all my life. The only one lying is you." She thrust a condemning finger nearly under Serafino's nose. "I cannot think what you hope to gain by defaming her this way, but whatever game you thought to play is over. Brother or no, you are no longer welcome here. Gather your belongings and leave before nightfall, or I will have my husband turn you out. And believe me when I say you will not care to be on the receiving end of his temper."

Serafino answered with a shrug of one shoulder. "Certainly, *signora,* I would not expect to remain beneath your roof after this. But I do not think I will be the only one suffering your husband's anger when he learns how my sister has duped you all." He lifted his brow at Lucianna. "Do you wish to tell them the truth, *cara,* or shall I?"

Sir Balduin continued to gaze at her with devotion and confidence through his perplexity, while Siri glared more furiously still at Serafino. But Lucianna knew what she must say. There was too much spite in Serafino's face to hope he might be driven from Vere Castle without exposing her. But this time, she would not be the only one disgraced by the truth.

"*Si,* I will tell them!" she flashed. "I will tell them how I am the daughter and the *sister* of a thief!"

That brought a rush of satisfyingly agitated color to Serafino's face. "Speak carefully, *cara,*" he said with quiet menace in his voice.

"Why?" she demanded. "If I am guilty, then we are guilty

together. You are the one who should have been careful, Serafino. This is not Venice. You have no friends here and I am not afraid of you anymore."

"That I see," he acknowledged, the dangerous glint returned to his eye. "However, I am not the one holding a stolen gem in my hand, and my father died a respectable man in his bed, while yours gasped his last while he swung from a hangman's rope."

She heard the sharp intake of Sir Balduin's breath and whirled towards him. "I did not steal this." She slapped the ring into his hand. "But Serafino speaks true of my father."

She did not know how she found the strength to meet Sir Balduin's eyes as she said it. The only expression she saw there was more bewilderment. It was Siri who once more protested.

"Lucianna, that is absurd. Your father was a merchant who died when you were a babe. Mama and Papà always said so."

Lucianna drew a breath that dragged painfully through her chest. She shifted her gaze to Siri, knowing that whatever she said next, she would find forgiveness there. She could not hope for the same in Sir Balduin's eyes, and she could not bear to watch devotion shrivel into horror and disgust.

"Your papà believed it," Lucianna said, "because your mama told him it was so, *carissima*, as she had told her own father and everyone else we knew. But we made it all up together, she and I, in the nunnery, because we did not wish to be parted when her father summoned her home."

Siri's lovely mouth fell agape at these words. Lucianna wondered if Sir Balduin's had done the same, or if disillusionment had begun to tighten his lips instead. She told herself that she hurried on for Elisabetta's sake, that her daughter might not think too hardly of her.

"In your mama's defense and mine, we did not then know the truth. We knew only that I had been left at the nunnery as a babe, a nameless foundling. It seemed a harmless game to play, until Serafino found me."

"I assure you," Serafino said, "that I was shocked to discover I had a sister, and one moreover who was posing to a life her birth did not entitle her to. I kept mum only out of respect for your mother, *signora*. Again and again I turned my eyes when my sister—my *half*-sister—betrayed her father's blood as she embezzled and defrauded to conceal her secret."

Oh, how smoothly he could lie!

"I hoped she had changed, that an honest man—" Serafino bowed towards Sir Balduin "—with his patience and love, might turn her to become an honest woman. But my hopes are dashed and once and for all, I wash my hands of you." He struck his palms together twice in Lucianna's direction, as though literally divesting them of something unclean. Then he turned to Siri. "I will be gone from here by nightfall. If my sister wishes to join me, I will escort her back to Venice. If not—well, I will attempt to defend her no longer. I leave her to the mercies of yourself and *Don* Triston."

Serafino spun on his heel, disdain jutting his chin in the air, and strode out of the chamber, leaving Lucianna alone to bear the blast of the tempest he had loosed.

Eleven

Lucianna endured the deafening silence that followed Serafino's departure until she could bear it no longer. She pulled her gaze away from the open doorway and turned to Siri.

"I must go with him," she murmured, "but not until I have told you the rest, *carissima*. May we retire to your chamber?"

Easier to confess it all to Siri and let her relay the story to Sir Balduin after Lucianna was gone. A coward's choice, but one she grasped at all the same.

Siri flung her arms passionately around her, slipping Lucianna just for a moment again into the past and that day twenty-nine years ago when Siri's mother had embraced her so fiercely after Serafino's revelation of her birth.

"I do not care what your beastly brother says," Siri cried. "You are my own dear Lucianna. That is all I need ever know. Nothing you could tell me could make me love you less."

Siri's loyalty, so like her mother's, brought tears again to Lucianna's eyes. "Still, I must tell you, *carissima*."

She thought she had whispered the words into Siri's ear, but they must have rasped through the lump in her throat for Sir Balduin said, "I think I deserve to hear it, too."

Lucianna winced at the stiffness in his voice. She turned her head slowly to look at him. Ah! Just as she had feared. His lips were drawn tight while his grey eyes no longer looked puzzled and devoted, but hard and grim. She wished Siri had been taller. She longed to shrink into the other woman's embrace, nay, she wished she might vanish clean away! But she had no choice but to shake herself free of Siri's protective love. He was right. She owed him the truth before she went.

"Then let her sit while she tells us," Siri said.

Lucianna had not realized that her face must be white until she felt Siri drawing her across the room to Sir Balduin's bed and felt how weakly her knees resisted when Siri nudged her to sit on the edge. One more glance revealed that Sir Balduin had crossed his arms forbiddingly across his chest. After that, Lucianna kept her gaze fastened again on Siri.

Lucianna told her haltingly of befriending her mother in the convent where Siri's grandfather had sent his daughter to be educated; of the sisterhood that had grown between her mother and Lucianna, and the plot they had woven to persuade Elisabetta's father to welcome Lucianna into his home so that she and Elisabetta might not be parted.

"We were so very young and it seemed harmless," Lucianna repeated. "And as Elisabetta often said when my conscience quickened, we did not know that the story about my parents was *not* true, as we knew nothing about them at all. We chose the name Fabio from an itinerate friar who stopped briefly at the abbey when we were girls. He said he hailed from Abruzzo, a region so far from Venice that we thought the name could never be traced to anyone who could prove it false." She did not tell Siri about her dream of Panfilo, the shining young man she had imagined as her father. All these years later, it still felt too painful to remember how foolish she had been to embrace a phantom hope.

She saw Siri toss a glance to one side—at Sir Balduin?— before she sat down beside Lucianna and reached out to hold her hand. Lucianna struggled to draw courage from the younger woman's clasp, even as she shrank from the stark silence than stretched from where Sir Balduin stood to the side of Lucianna's vision.

She forced herself to continue. "At first, Elisabetta said that we should never be parted, that when she married, she would take me for her companion to her husband's house. So many men came to court her, for she was beautiful and spirited and intelligent, and her father had wealth enough to deck her out in the finest silks and jewels. As her father hoped, many of her suitors were rich and noble, but some of them were of her own merchant class, and when they saw that her father frowned on them, they began to turn their attentions to me. I had never dared think of marriage, for I had not a *denaro* to my name, but one day Elisabetta exclaimed that it was not fair, that I was pretty and well mannered and well educated too, and why should I not have a husband of my own? I reminded her that I had no dowry. And then I am afraid I cried, for a handsome young man named Vincenzo Mirolli had begun to show particular affection for me, but I knew he could never accept a dowerless wife."

She heard a stirring from Sir Balduin's direction and paused to hold her breath, but he did not speak. The question of a dowry had never risen between them. Although she had made no objection when Triston's household had taken to calling her "lady," she had always assumed that Sir Balduin and everyone had known her dependent on Siri with no independent wealth of her own. Had she been mistaken? Had he misinterpreted the gowns that Siri had bought for her as a reflection of personal affluence? Then perhaps the rest of the story would be a relief for him, a release from an obligation he had offered her under a false belief.

Lucianna gave a doleful sniff and ran the back of her hand against her nose to hide her trembling lips until she stilled them enough to continue.

"If I had known what your mother intended, *carissima*, I would have stopped her. But she disappeared for hours one afternoon, and when she returned she showed me a small wooden casket filled with silver. She had sold her finest pearl necklace, a very expensive gift from her father, and declared the coins she had received for them should be my dowry to marry Vincenzo. I protested. Although she insisted the necklace was hers to do with as she pleased, it felt like theft to me. I told her I would not accept the coins, but she laughed and said that it was too late, she had already shown them to Vincenzo and that he had agreed them sufficient to satisfy his father's expectations for his bride."

Siri sat listening patiently, but the silence from Sir Balduin grew intolerable. Lucianna bounced up from the bed, careful not to catch his eye, yet unable to stand still. She bent to pick up one of the tunics tumbled onto the floor.

"I was a foolish, foolish girl." She laid the tunic on the bed and tried to smooth out its wrinkles, but her fingers shook too hard to succeed. "I thought myself in love, and so I let your mother convince me to accept her 'gift.' Vincenzo asked for my hand. Your grandfather performed the role of my 'deceased' father and granted it to him, accepting Elisabetta's explanation that the nuns had kept my 'dowry' in their own safe keeping until an eligible man wished to marry me."

She folded the still creased garment in half, tucking the sleeves in skillfully so that the lines in the cloth should at least grow no worse, then scooped up a rumpled smock and repeated the procedure.

"But you did not marry Vincenzo," Siri said as Lucianna allowed herself to succumb to the increasingly soothing rhythm of gathering and folding Sir Balduin's scattered clothes. Somehow the busyness of the motions helped to keep more tears from her eyes.

Siri gave a tiny gasp. "Or did you?"

Lucianna thought she heard a similar sharp indrawn breath from Sir Balduin, but she had bent down to snag a pair of his hose and could not have seen his expression from her position, even if she had wanted to.

"No, *carissima*, I did not for it was the very next day that Serafino revealed himself to me."

She shook out the hose. How long had Sir Balduin been

wearing these with a hole in the heel? She almost snapped a rebuke at him for enduring a flaw she could have mended in minutes, then caught herself with a pang. She was not his wife, nor ever would be. If he chose to deck himself out in an entire wardrobe full of rifts and rents, it was no longer her affair. Nevertheless, she folded the hose as tenderly as she had the other garments.

She took a pair of steps to reach for a tumbled surcote, then stumbled with dismay when Sir Balduin finally spoke roughly from the other side of the room.

"Serafino, who claimed the Fabio name so proud that I must marry you to preserve your reputation. But if the name is a lie for you, then I presume it was a lie for him, as well?"

She clutched the surcote to her breast as though it might prove some shield against his glare as she turned slowly to finally meet Sir Balduin's gaze.

He was not glaring, though his eyes were very hard.

"*Si*," she said. "His name is Amorosi. Mine I do not know, for I never knew my father and the record only noted him as Giovanni the thief."

Sir Balduin's lips parted as if he would say more, but she held up a hand to forestall him.

"*No*, let me tell the rest, then you may condemn me all at once." She rushed on when Sir Balduin looked as though he meant to argue. "Serafino was a woolmonger's son who sometimes did business with Elisabetta's father. The day after my betrothal was announced, Serafino told me he was my half-brother. He showed me irrefutable proof."

She recalled as vividly as if it were yesterday scanning the words of the parchment roll that told of her father's trial, conviction, and sentence. Heard again the small *click* of the silver frame springing free of her mother's ruby brooch with her mother's name scratched into the jewel's back. Heard once more Serafino's voice— "*Antonia Amorosi was your mother, dear one, but he was your father.*" And then the worst memory of all: Mother Rosalba's confirmation and the words the nun had shouted after Lucianna as she had fled in horror from the revelation: *"Theft and wantonness run in your blood. It is not too late to return to us to spare shame to those in the world who have come to care for you."*

She had held that shame at bay for nearly thirty years. She had never been wanton, and she had never directly stolen anything, but again and again the guilt had engulfed her as she had given Serafino "gifts" to go away. If she had not inherited thievery in her blood, her father had certainly willed her cowardice, and her mother too much pride to confess it.

But now, there was no place left to hide.

Humiliating as it was, Lucianna repeated the rest of the story. "When Serafino was ten-years-old, one of their servants stole some of his father's property and ran away. The thief was caught by the city watch, tried, and hanged. All the property was recovered save for a ruby brooch, which they said he must have sold before his capture." She began to nervously pleat the cloth of the surcote she was holding. "There followed in Serafino's home a round of terrible quarrels between his parents, during which he claimed to have overheard such words as—" Lucianna's breath shook on a pause "—'seduction,' 'thief's brat,' and 'by-blow' flung by his father at his mother."

She felt a sickened roil in her stomach and dropped her gaze to the pile of still ungathered clothes at her feet. "Then his mother shut herself away for a very long time. When next Serafino saw her, she had a baby in her arms and she bade Serafino accompany her to visit the nuns of the *convento de Santa Caterina.* Serafino said his mother told him to stand watch while she spoke to the nuns, but he became frightened because it was dark and started after her. He saw his mother lay the baby gently on the doorstep of the abbey, then draw a brooch from beneath her cloak and pin it to the baby's blanket. Then she rang the abbey bell and hurried away, sweeping Serafino before her when she found him so near."

Lucianna tried to smooth out the creases she had pressed

into the rumpled surcote, and finally felt the stab of recognition. The blue cloth with its swirling pattern of yellow and red embroidery, the one that brought out the hint of blue in his grey eyes—she held the surcote Sir Balduin had worn the night he had asked her to marry him. She turned and tossed it onto the bed as though it suddenly burned her. When she lifted her gaze again, it was to the safety once more of Siri's eyes.

"My own unknown mother had left me a ruby brooch when she abandoned me to the nuns. When Serafino saw it holding a mantle against my shoulder, he said he knew it at once. It was the brooch the servant-thief had taken that had never been found. I did not want to believe it at first, but Serafino took me back to the convent where the reverend mother verified his story, for my mother had called her and confessed to her the truth before she died. Serafino said he would keep quiet if I would pay off a debt he had incurred."

Lucianna's stomach continued to feel like heaving, molten lead. "I was frightened and angry and knew not what to say. I knew that Cosimo Gallo would not keep me in his house if he learned the truth, no matter how Elisabetta begged. Elisabetta knew it, too. So we paid Serafino. Again and again, we paid him to go away and again and again he returned demanding more.

Siri must have seen how painfully Lucianna had begun to wring her hands, for she stood up from the bed. She picked up a girdle from the floor that had been tossed in such a manner as had left it in a knot and gave it to Lucianna. Lucianna silently blessed her and turned her nervousness to plucking at the knot.

"Serafino came again a week before my wedding. Your father, *carissima*, was newly arrived from Poitou on a pilgrimage to Jerusalem. Your grandfather often aided such pilgrims in arranging a sea route to the Holy Land. Walter Geraud was like you in his golden beauty, but he was also generous and good. Without her father's knowledge, and certainly against his will, Elisabetta and Walter fell in love. I had seen the looks of affection growing between them while Walter and his party awaited the transport ship. Thinking he would soon be gone and grieve your mother, I encouraged her to spend what time she could with him before his departure. And so, the next time Serafino found me, I was alone."

The more Lucianna pulled at the knot in the girdle, the tighter it seemed to grow. What force had Sir Balduin flung it with to tangle it so badly?

She immediately regretted thinking his name, for it sent her mind racing with fresh imaginings of how he watched her while she spoke. With horror? Revulsion? Pity? It was almost a relief to lose herself again in the story.

"As always, Serafino demanded money. But I had grown weary and angry with him. I had injured a finger and consequently had had no embroidery to sell, and I refused to let him squeeze another coin or jewel from your mother. I lost my temper with him as I often did, but this time Elisabetta was not there to hush me and pay him against my protests. I told him there would be no more. He replied that if I did not give him something, he would tell Vincenzo that I was the baseborn daughter of a thief. I did not believe he would dare. I told him to go to perdition, for there would be no more jewels or silver."

The knot came loose so abruptly that it startled her briefly from the memory. But the pain washed back the next instant.

"So he did it. Serafino told Vincenzo about my birth and Vincenzo shunned me. Elisabetta persuaded Vincenzo not to repeat the tale, but he severed our betrothal and I never saw him again." Tears blurred her eyes, not for Vincenzo's loss, but for the loss of the grey-haired knight who stood just beyond her vision, who had made her feel more cherished and loved than she had ever felt with the young, vivacious, flamboyant Vincenzo. Lucianna paused a moment to regain her composure, then smoothed the girdle and set it on the bed with the other clothing she had neatened. "After that, we never dared challenge Serafino again."

"Is that why you never married?" Siri asked. Lucianna saw her eyes slide sideways, and knew she glanced again at Sir Balduin.

"*Si.*"

She would not tell them how she had covered her hurt by throwing herself into the refuge of the identity she and Elisabetta had invented. How she had held her head a bit too high and hinted that Vincenzo had been unworthy of her, for he had left the city after their break and could not betray her or defend himself. She had wept for him one single, bitter night, then cast a wall about her heart, veneered with pride and disdain to keep any man from too sorely tempting her again. Until one day she had realized she wore the pride too easily and wondered if, as Mother Rosalba had said, it had always been in her nature and her blood. Too late by then. She was Lucianna the proud, the haughty.

Now she was Lucianna the humiliated and disgraced.

Her hands twitched for something new to do. She saw a series of scattered shoes and moved to gather them into an orderly line on the floor.

"Your mother soon afterwards ran away with your father," she said to Siri as she worked. "She reconciled quickly with your grandfather, disappointed though he was that his beautiful daughter had married a simple craftsman. Walter did not complete his pilgrimage. But you know that part of the story."

She set two half-boots side by side, turning down their tops to expose their green lining. She would not truly have minded stitching a flourishing pattern against the green. It would have pleased her to bring envy to her husband's boots. She sighed.

"Your mother took me with her into her new home. Serafino haunted us even there, but we had not as much to give him and he knew it. Still, he continued to blackmail what he could from us without your father's knowledge. Then strangely, he disappeared shortly after your parents died so near to one another. Perhaps he knew they did not leave you and your brother enough wealth to be worth extorting. But when you married Alessandro and became a *donna*, once more he appeared and the nightmare began again."

Lucianna did not expect Sir Balduin to believe her—the mere whiff of her sordid parentage had been enough to disgust Vincenzo and frighten him away—but she turned to Siri and insisted, "*Carissima*, despite what Serafino said here today, I never, never stole from you or Alessandro—not directly. But you gifted me with so many fine gowns and jewels that those I sometimes gave to Serafino to sell. You were so innocent and trusting that when I told you I'd torn or lost them, you merely gave me more. Then Serafino would come again and threaten and I would give him those. And each time I did, it felt like theft and I remembered that I was the baseborn daughter of a thief and I hated myself." Her eyes stung bitterly again.

Siri stepped towards her, but Lucianna stopped her with a thrust out hand.

"*No*, stay. It was weak of me, and dishonorable and contemptible. But I was so afraid of losing you." A hot, wet trickle started down her cheek. "You were all I had left of Elisabetta. I had helped her to run off with your father. I held her hand as she gave birth to your brother, and then to you. I helped her nurse every illness you and your brother bore. And when she was gone, it was my arms that held and comforted you in your grief."

In our grief.

"As you held me again when Alessandro died, and then my brother." Siri's eyes shone with a reflection of Lucianna's tears. "I wish you had not been afraid to tell me. I would never, never have blamed you. You did not need to carry this burden alone."

"If Alessandro had known, he would have cast me from his house."

Siri's eyes flashed at that. "He would not! I would never have let him—"

"You were scarcely more than a child, *carissima,* you could not have stopped him. I could not bear to be parted from you. So I let Serafino endlessly blackmail me. When your brother died and his will sent us here to Poitou, I thought *infine!* At last I will be free of Serafino! But somehow he found me even here."

Lucianna whisked the tears impatiently from her cheeks, then fisted her fingers until her nails dug into her palms, anger at Serafino flaring against her despair.

"He frightened me at first into giving him my embroidered black gown, but then I said *non più.* No more. I would not let him wring so much as another *denaro* from me or from someone I love. So now I will leave you, and take Serafino with me. You do not need me any longer, *carissima.*"

"I will always need you," Siri said passionately. "Now that we know the truth about Serafino, he cannot threaten you any further. There is no reason for you to go now."

There was still one. Lucianna could not bear to remain in a household where she would be forced to see Sir Balduin and have the pain of his loss renewed in her heart every day. Even when he left Vere to serve as castellan of Dauvillier Castle, she would most certainly hear his name still spoken on Triston's lips, would be required to avoid him when Triston summoned him back to report or counsel him from time to time. No, she could not live like this, grieving for a man she loved, knowing him still so near, feeling his revulsion for her stretching between their castles. And if he found someone else to love and marry, someone who would not bring disgrace to his name— Lucianna dug her nails deeper to stop herself from weeping anew at the anguished vision.

She guessed that Siri had read her thoughts when the blue eyes slid towards Sir Balduin again. Lucianna struggled to control her shuddering breath, then turned her head to gaze at him, too.

His grey eyes blazed as she had only seen them do once before, when anger had provoked him to draw his sword in a hallowed church to defend Siri from the baron who sought to abduct her. Lucianna had thought then, *This must be the look he carries into battle.* Only the fire sprang at her now, not an offending baron. She tried to speak, but what more could she say? She had too much lingering pride to beg for a forgiveness she knew herself unworthy and unlikely to receive.

Siri spoke in a pleading voice. "Sir Balduin—"

But he cut her off with a brusque shake of his head. He looked down briefly at his grandmother's ring. Then he yanked it from the chain, flung the latter on the bed beside the pile of clothes Lucianna had laid there, and crammed the ring onto his finger. Any lingering thread of hope that Lucianna had nourished snapped.

"Your pardon, Lady Siri." He bowed to his young mistress. "I have a matter to attend to."

He strode from the room without another glance at Lucianna, just as Vincenzo had walked out of her life nearly thirty years ago.

Twelve

Sir Balduin swore silently when he encountered Triston coming up the stairs that Sir Balduin had begun to descend.

"I was on my way to find you," Triston said. "What is this about Lucianna leaving with her brother?"

Sir Balduin struggled to steady the angry breaths heaving his chest. "Where heard you that?"

"From Serafino. He asked me if he might take some food for their journey. He is in the kitchen gathering some now."

Sir Balduin wondered if this reddish haze at the edges of his vision was how the world looked when Triston fell into one of his volatile bouts of temper. He did not even realize he had brushed past his young master until he heard Triston call out after him, "Where are you going?"

Sir Balduin did not answer. Too many curses hovered on his tongue to be certain one of them might not slip out at any delay that Triston caused him.

A smoky haze still hung in the kitchen, lingering with the fading aromas of the dishes that had been served at dinner only a few hours before, but Serafino was alone in the room. It looked like food was not the only thing on his mind. While a basket sat on a table, spilling over with loaves of bread, fruit, pasties, tarts, and other easily transportable foodstuffs, he held a bag into which Sir Balduin saw him drop a slotted spoon that clanged against some metal object already inside, followed by a small iron pot he plucked from the cold stove.

Serafino had a frying pan in his hand when Sir Balduin said, "You'll break your teeth on that. Iron makes a poor dinner, sir."

Serafino started and turned from the stove, but recovered quickly from his surprise. "*Don* Triston gave me leave—"

"—to depart with some food from our kitchen," Sir Balduin finished. He crossed the floor with his limping gait and swiped the bag from Serafino's hand, opening the neck to gaze inside. "None of these items look edible to me. They might earn you several handfuls of silver, though." He looked back at Serafino, silently villifying the eyes so near in shade to Lucianna's. "I suppose this should not surprise me?"

"You mistake, *signore*," Serafino said, politely but firmly retrieving the bag. "I borrow these, merely. I am not a rich man and I refuse to beg for—how do you say? *Carità?*"

"*Charité*," Sir Balduin growled. "It is not so different from your own tongue, sir." Unlike that blasted word for patience he could not recall how to pronounce. Italian's odd and inconsistent Cs, their rolling Rs, their inexplicable Zs—he could hardly be blamed for his confusion. But this word was perfectly understandable in both their languages.

Serafino smiled, as though Sir Balduin did not know he spoke French almost as neatly as Lucianna did. "*Si.* Charity. I will not beg it of *Don* Triston after my sister has so wickedly deceived him. Our journey is long, and it may be that I will not be able to afford the cost of an inn for us both every night. Should necessity confine us to more humble refuge, I take these items merely that we may prepare a few simple meals. As soon as we are back in Venice I will resume my wool trade, and at the first opportunity I will pay a trustworthy messenger to return these."

"Liar." The smile faded from Serafino's face as the bald word burst from Sir Balduin. "You intend to sell those to indulge the vices Lucianna has refused any longer to support.

Likely you will drag her home in rags—if you do not simply abandon her. I would not put it past your black heart."

Serafino went very stiff. "*Signore*, whatever Lucianna has told you of me in an attempt to lessen in your sight her own guilt is, at the very least, a vast distortion of my misdeeds. I may have, on a rare occasion, requested a small loan from her. But it was she who chose to maintain her silence after I revealed to her the truth of her birth so that she might not lose the many privileges she had acquired by beguiling a friendship with a wealthy merchant's daughter. Perhaps I was wrong to help her maintain her deceit, but in truth, I saw it as a kindness. Imagine what her future would have been had Cosimo Gallo thrust her out, a young, pretty woman, into the streets of Venice?"

"Oh, I do not doubt in the least that is the very fear you preyed upon with her. A kindness? Pah! You are a scurrilous bully of a scoundrel. To call yourself her brother is to befoul the word."

Serafino colored. "You are overwrought, *signore*, for which I cannot blame you. It was most certainly a terrible shock to learn how the woman you loved has deceived you. I cannot express to you the depths of my own disappointment, but what can one do? 'Blood will out,' as they say, and I fear she will always be a thief's daughter. The moment I saw your ring in her hand and realized she had returned to her pilfering ways—"

Sir Balduin snapped his fist into Serafino's face and watched with satisfaction as the blow threw him into a sprawl across the stove.

"*Che diavolo!*" Serafino exclaimed, dropping the frying pan so he could press his hand to the eye that Sir Balduin had clouted shut.

Sir Balduin resisted the impulse to close the other in similar fashion. Whatever whim of fate had thought it amusing to match the beautiful hue of Lucianna's eyes with this dastard's should be laughing a little less gleefully now.

"Malign her again," Sir Balduin warned, "and next time I will break your nose. You may well thank the heavens that I am not wearing my sword."

The eye that was not swelling behind Serafino's palm flared with alarm. "Malign her? My only sin was in not telling you of her iniquitous character as soon as I arrived. For that, *si*, I confess myself at fault, and for that I will forgive this unwarranted attack of yours. But *signore*, it was not I who attempted to steal your ring. You saw her for yourself —"

"She had no need to steal my ring," Sir Balduin cut him off. "I had given it to her freely. She could have fled with you and it in the middle of the night if she'd wished to make off with it, instead of flinging it back at me."

Sir Balduin took a step forward, prompting Serafino to scurry away from the stove, but not before he bent down to scoop up the frying pan again as he rolled his one good eye apprehensively in Sir Balduin's direction. Sir Balduin's blood had begun a familiar pumping, reminding him of the days before his injury when he had ridden into battle at the sides of the masters of Vere. Truly, his palm itched for the feel of a sword hilt.

"You, on the other hand," Sir Balduin said, stalking Serafino through the kitchen, "comforted me in the garden while I bemoaned that disastrous song I sang to her. You asked, as I recall, rather probing questions about my means to support a wife."

Serafino darted behind a large wine barrel. Sir Balduin stopped, allowing him the barrier as he continued.

"Then you embraced me with the assurance that you would help plead my cause with her. The ring was most certainly still around my neck when I rose from bed yester-morning. I recall feeling its weight against my chest as I dined." Or more precisely during his melodic debacle. "So it must have been sometime after I retreated to the garden that it disappeared. Had a servant found the ring, it would have been promptly returned to me, for Triston has made a thorough sweep of the corrupt hirelings of his father's day. But your embrace—it startled me. Sufficiently so that I suspect I did not notice when you undid the chain's clasp and slipped chain and ring together from my neck."

A swift sidestep by Sir Balduin flushed Serafino out from behind the barrel and sent him backing towards the table with the basket.

"But *signore*," Serafino insisted, "if that were true, you would have found it in my possession, not in my sister's. It is more likely that she slid it from your neck while she held you distracted with the kisses *Donna* Siri and I discovered you engaged in in your chamber. *Si*, it was immediately after that that we found it in her hand."

"That is impossible, since it was missing when I retired to my bed last night and I spent the entire night and half the morning upending my chamber in search of it. If it had fallen off there, I would have found it. Which means Lucianna could not have uncovered it in my chamber to steal it, because it wasn't there."

Panic shone clearly now in Serafino's unbruised eye. "But—but you must have overlooked it, despite your search. How else would it have come into her possession?"

"That is a very good question," Sir Balduin admitted. "And it is one I will ask her as soon as I am done thrashing you from head to toe."

With his gaze fixed on the fresh fist Sir Balduin was forming, Serafino bumped right into the table. He knocked over a crock of flour into a platter of gingerbread undoubtedly intended for the lady of the castle, and splashed a pot of milk into the basket of food for his travels.

Seeing Serafino's distraction, Sir Balduin grasped him by the front of his surcote, intending to pull him into a more open space to permit the promised trouncing. Serafino reacted with a gasping curse and swung the frying pan at Sir Balduin's head. Sir Balduin ducked. Serafino leapt past him, but Sir Balduin caught his shoulder and spun him back. The frying pan swooped again at Sir Balduin's skull. Again Sir Balduin dodged. This time when he straightened he landed his fist in Serafino's other eye.

"That is for breaking her heart with Vincenzo Mirolli," Sir Balduin growled, heroically choking down his jealousy of Lucianna's first love while simultaneously cursing and thanking the unknown man for spurning her. Had he not, she would never have entered Sir Balduin's life.

Serafino scrambled up from the floor bleary-eyed with another wild swing of the pan. Sir Balduin evaded it again, then plowed his fist into Serafino's chin.

"That is for all the years you bullied and terrified her with threats to as good as throw her into the streets if she did not bow to your villainous demands."

The table broke Serafino's fall that time, though it sent the gingerbread flying off its platter. Serafino recovered to make one last wobbling attempt to defend himself with his kitchen weapon. This time Sir Balduin averted the attack easily. He heard and felt a satisfying *crack* as his fist connected with Serafino's nose. Serafino dropped howling to the floor, the frying pan clattering free as his hands flew to try to staunch the blood flowing from his nostrils.

"And that one is for myself," Sir Balduin said. "When I think how near I came to losing her because of you —"

He broke off, his voice shaking with emotion. For it had all become clear to Sir Balduin in his chamber when Lucianna had told her story, sealed on his heart when she had said, "*Non più.* No more. I would not let him wring so much as another *denaro* from me or someone I love."

She had meant him, Sir Balduin knew it. It had not been Siri's judgment Lucianna feared as she revealed her birth and Serafino's extortion. Again and again she had kept her gaze on Siri because she knew herself safe in the young woman's love. It nearly cleft Sir Balduin's heart in two that she had not felt herself safe in his.

Serafino's probing questions in the garden about Sir Balduin's emerald ring, the silver needles, and his future prospects as castellan of Dauvillier Castle stood adequate proof that the knave had planned to exploit him if he married Lucianna. It had taken the tigress spirit Sir Balduin had always admired in her for Lucianna to defy this man she had stood in fear of for nearly thirty years. Through all her painful rebuffs of the last few weeks, the one thing she had never done was deny that she still loved Sir Balduin, her passion reaffirmed by her ardent return of his kiss in his chamber. Her rejection of their marriage had been an attempt to protect him from her reprobate brother, and to slip away from Poitou before Sir Balduin learned why.

"Stop blubbering like a baby," Sir Balduin said as Serafino continued whimpering over his broken nose. Sir Balduin picked up the basket dripping with milk and thrust it with its bountiful foodstuffs into Serafino's arms. "That should get you well over the Norman border. See that you send back the horse when you get to Rouen, unless you wish me to dispatch a guard after you to drag you back as a horse thief."

An ironic end that would be, he thought, if Serafino found himself at the end of a rope like Lucianna's sire.

From the shudder that shook Serafino, the same prospect appeared to occur to him.

"Here, you may take this along too, since you seem so fond of it." Sir Balduin picked up the frying pan and dropped it in Serafino's lap. The cook might chide Sir Balduin's generosity, but two more skillets lay in plain view about the kitchen. "You may sell it after you return the horse to finance what you can of the rest of your journey. After that, you and your despicable wits are on your own. Only I warn you not to let me see your face again, for I'll not content myself with blackening your eyes and cracking your nose next time."

Serafino groaned, his hand fluttering gingerly over his red, bulbous, still-bloodied nose. "What about Lucianna?" he muttered.

"That is up to her. If she still wishes to return to Venice, be assured she will do so with every comfort and honor Lady Siri can bestow on her, along with a trustworthy guard that shall keep her safe from fiends like you forevermore."

Sir Balduin left the kitchen, then checked his angry strides, startled to discover Triston just without in the passageway that linked the kitchen to the hall.

"Sir!"

Triston lifted one of his ebony brows. "Is it settled?"

"Is what settled?"

Triston's gaze dropped briefly to the bruises on Sir Balduin's knuckles before returning to Sir Balduin's face with a bit of a glint in his eye. "I did not catch all the words you flung, but I know the sounds of a fistfight when I hear it. I gathered you did not need any assistance from me."

Sir Balduin rubbed his knuckles. He had not realized they were sore until Triston drew his attention to them. He hesitated. He supposed he would have to tell Triston everything eventually. But he had one more person to "settle" things with, first.

"If it would not be inconvenient, sir, might we lend Serafino a few knights to see him safely"—and permanently—"away from Vere?"

Triston nodded. "Certainly. Will Lady Lucianna be accompanying him?"

Sir Balduin felt his own brows snap down. "She will not."

Triston smiled. "She is staying then?"

Sir Balduin sighed and his shoulders sagged a little. "That I do not yet know."

Thirteen

I must go with him," Lucianna insisted. "Let me pass, *carissima*, so that I may collect a few things." She would take only her embroidery and a few of her humbler gowns, just enough to feign respectability on the journey. Surely the heavens would not condemn her for clinging to one last fragile strand of pride, to return to Venice modest but comely, rather than with the open abasement her birth deserved of shabby skirts and tangled hair.

"Do not speak nonsense," Siri said, firmly blocking Lucianna from exiting Sir Balduin's chamber. "You are not going anywhere, least of all with that wretch that calls himself your brother. Besides, you promised you would stay until after the baby was born." She crossed her arms with that stubbornness that had always lain beneath her soft beauty, resting them above her swollen belly.

Lucianna was spent with tears and had little energy left to continue this quarrel, but she had made up her mind and even weary, she could be stubborn too. "That was before today, before Serafino made me tell you my shame. I cannot stay now, you know I cannot."

She had sat weeping on Sir Balduin's bed at his abrupt departure from the chamber. She had known he would spurn her when he learned the truth and thought she had braced herself for the hurt. But the anguish she had suffered when she had made the decision to leave him paled at the agony of his rejection. He may as well have taken his dagger and ripped out her heart as have bolted from her presence in what could only have been disgust and loathing. Vincenzo's desertion had stung, but it had not left her aching and throbbing as if from a physical blow.

This day would obliterate all her precious memories of the past—Sir Balduin's initial awkwardness at courting her, his persistence when she had sought at first to imperiously dismiss him, the surprising whimsy in his smiles that had gradually worn down her resistance, the way his kisses had beguiled her, his valiant attempts to learn Italian to please her even though the words tangled his tongue, the courage he had shown in defending Siri when faced with a half-dozen swords at his breast— Every action, every word, every expression that had made her love him, ruined now by the memory of this day that could never be wiped from her mind and heart because she would always know he had not wiped it from his.

She had dried her tears slowly, but at length they had ceased. It was hard to imagine ever finding peace, but if such a refuge lay anywhere for her, it must be in the *convento de Santa Caterina*. Mother Rosalba would have passed on years ago. Perhaps a kinder abbess had taken her place, but even if she, too, were cold, Lucianna was no longer a child to be frightened or intimidated. At least there in the convent, she could still nourish sweet reminiscences of her girlhood with Elisabetta.

"Lucianna." Siri reached across to take her hands. "Nothing has changed about you in my eyes, not so much as a whit."

Lucianna's breast warmed with gratitude, even as a chill trickled up her spine. "Perhaps not in yours. But in *Don* Triston's and *Signor* Balduin's . . ."

"Triston will drub Serafino from the castle when he learns what your brother has done," Siri declared, but Lucianna saw the way she faltered on the rest. "And Sir Balduin . . . I am sure he only needs a little time, to . . . to understand . . ."

150

She trailed off, for Lucianna knew Siri had witnessed with her the anger in Sir Balduin's eyes before he had stalked out of the chamber.

Siri's fingers tightened on Lucianna's. "Just stay until the baby comes," she pled. "I still need you for that. Please."

Lucianna choked back a lingering hiccough of despair from her tears, but she refused to weep further. "*Carissima*, I do not see how I can. To live within the same walls as he for another four weeks—" Her voice broke in spite of herself. "Hide in my chamber I will not, but to walk the passageways, the hall, the garden with downcast eyes lest I glimpse him, fearing what he must think each time he sees me— I cannot bear that, however much I love you." She swept Siri into her arms and kissed the pallor that had replaced the roses in the young woman's cheeks. "*Don* Triston would never let harm come to you. He will surround you with wise and comforting *matrone*. You are no longer a child, *carissima*, and you do not need me at your side as you bear your first babe."

"I do," Siri whispered, her shoulders shaking softly with tears of her own. "I do not want strange matrons around me. I want *you*." Then she pulled away and wiped her wet cheeks. "But that is selfish of me, when I know how you hurt. I *do* know, Lucianna. I do."

Lucianna did not doubt her. She had stood witness to Siri's own anguish in her long battle to win Triston's love. Because Lucianna had withheld her approval of Triston at first had not made her ache the less for Siri's grief, nor had she rebuked Siri when Siri had once attempted to flee from her pain.

Siri said, her voice gruff but firm, "I will not try to dissuade you again. But do not go tonight and do not go with Serafino. Wait until I talk to Triston."

"No, *carissima*, please. I do not wish *Don* Triston to know until I am gone. He will be angry—"

"He will not!" Siri protested.

"*Si*, but he will. He will think as *Signor* Balduin does of me. You will try to defend me, and it will lead to a quarrel between you. I do not wish that. Just let me go in peace."

"But you cannot go alone. Let me arrange an escort for you, and —"

A footfall cut Siri off. Lucianna's face numbed at a fresh draining of blood at the sight of Sir Balduin, but before she could stop herself, her chin thrust up in challenge. As it did so, she remembered again Mother Rosalba's words and thought of the woman who had given her birth. Had Antonia Amorosi been as haughty and imperious as Mother Rosalba had said? Had it been a lofty, disdainful spirit that had prompted Antonia to reject her helpless, if misbegotten child, and leave her on the doorstep of a convent on a bitter cold winter's night, rather than endure the dishonor of the babe's existence?

Lucianna did not wish to be such a woman as that, yet a defensive pride was all she had left to cling to as she gazed into Sir Balduin's eyes.

"We were just leaving," she said, exquisitely aware in spite of her defiant posture of the embarrassment of being caught lingering in his chamber. "I thought I might finish making some order of this jumble before departing, but the task was impossible. Men! I suppose it says much about you that you choose to live amidst such disarray as this."

She would have swept out of the room, but his tall frame blocked her retreat across the threshold.

"I went to your chamber, but you were not there," he said. Something flickered in his grey eyes, but he glanced at Siri before Lucianna could try to identify what it signified. "Your pardon, my lady, but may I speak to the Lady Lucianna alone?"

Siri held fast to Lucianna's hand and waited for Lucianna to determine her own response.

"I think there is nothing left to say between us, *signore*," Lucianna said.

Sir Balduin's gaze remained on Siri. After a moment, to Lucianna's surprise, Siri's fingers slid away and she moved towards the doorway.

"I will be right outside," she promised. "You have only to call if you want me."

Sir Balduin stepped aside and Siri slipped out of the room. He closed the door with a soft *click* behind her. Lucianna stiffened, astonished at Siri's departure, but she told herself sternly there was nothing left to fear. He could not hurt her any deeper than he already had.

Sir Balduin wandered about the room, scooping up tumbled garments as he went. "I assure you, I am not always such a sloven, as you put it."

Her gaze caressed each familiar limping step, each dip and straightening of his muscular body as he gathered the clothes, the ripple in his grey hair, the strong, stolid profile tanned and creased from his long soldier's life. He bent to snag a green tunic with one finger. Surely it was only the dimming afternoon light that tricked her into thinking she saw his hand shake?

He hesitated, his arms filled with clothes, then crossed to the bed and dropped them in a heap next to the pile Lucianna had folded. "Did I hear Lady Siri say she was arranging an escort for you?"

She shifted her gaze quickly to the window as he turned to face her. "*Si*. It is generous of her, but not necessary. I will be quite safe in my brother's company."

Sir Balduin muttered something beneath his breath. He rarely swore in her presence but the muffled word, though indistinct, bore such a blasphemous hint that it startled her into glancing at him.

"Your brother." He spat it from his mouth as though the words fouled his tongue.

"*Si*," she said sharply. "I will repeat it in Italian so that it does not soil your ears as well. *Mio fratello*. He is waiting for me. Siri has agreed that I might take my embroidery and a few travelling gowns, so I am not stealing from her and *Don Triston*. I must go gather them if we are to leave before nightfall."

She started towards the now unguarded door, but Sir Balduin's next words stopped her.

"Serafino has already left." She turned to see Sir Balduin's face scrunch up in disgust. "*Serafino, sérafin*. It mean angelic in both our tongues. His parents would have done better to name him *Diable*. Or how would you say it? *Diavolo?*"

Lucianna recalled that he had heard her fling that epithet at a few of Siri's early suitors who had courted her more in lust than in love. Lucianna had thrown it a few times at Triston, too, before he had won her trust.

She bristled, feeling Sir Balduin's verbal dart pierce herself alongside her brother. "And how should the nuns have named me? Lucianna means light. Perhaps you will prefer to remember me as Bugiarda or Ladra?" *Liar. Thief.*

"I do not know those words," Sir Balduin said. "And from the fire in your face, I suspect it would be best to allow me to retain my ignorance."

His mouth curved upward as he said it. How dare he mock her with a smile? She whirled towards the door and had her hand on the latch before she remembered the rest of his speech. She swiveled her head to glare at him.

"What do you mean Serafino has left? He would not leave Vere without me." Surely not? He would be loitering about, hoping that Siri would heap Lucianna with parting gifts that he could seize and sell when they were gone.

"A pair of Triston's knights have escorted him from the castle. They will have seen him well clear of the manor by now."

"You told *Don* Triston?" She rounded on Sir Balduin, a panicked anger flooding through her. "You could not wait until I was gone before sharing my humiliation with him? Oh! Of all the things I ever thought of you, I never thought you spiteful!" She had resolved not to shed another tear, but her eyes burned again in defiance of her will. "I expected you to hate me, I *deserve* for you to hate me, but this?"

"Hate you?" Sir Balduin gasped.

Hurt and fury drove her on. "You know *Don* Triston's temper. He will fling me from the castle as he flung Serafino. I do not care for that—I do not!—but if he casts me out before I say goodbye to Siri it will break the last corner of my heart."

"So it is only Siri it will grieve you to leave?"

Something edged Sir Balduin's voice. She might have thought it bitterness, had she not known that to be impossible.

"The one person left on earth to still love me? *Si*, it will grieve me to leave her. But I do not expect you to understand."

She set her hand to the latch again, but Sir Balduin's palm slapped against the boards of the door holding it fast shut. Even knowing how swiftly he could move in spite of his limp, his sudden appearance at her side took her aback.

"Then do not go." His voice fell in a gruff breath on her ear. "Stay here with Siri. With us." His hand slid down the door until the found and lightly covered her fingers. "With me."

The air tangled in her throat at his touch. "Do not mock me," she whispered. "It is cruel." Spiteful and now callous to her pain? How had he hidden such facets of his character from her?

"Mock you?" She would not look at him, but it sounded like his own breath caught. "In truth, you are the most befuddling woman. Siri is not the only one who loves you, and though I know I can never rival her in your heart, I will content myself with that unbroken corner you speak of if you will let me, while Siri helps you mend the rest."

The burning tears leaked free as she struggled with his meaning. "It is not Siri who broke my heart. She is not the one who walked out on me."

This time there was no mistaking his curse. "Serafino. But he is not worth your tears." Sir Balduin's hand brushed against her wet cheek. "He may be your brother, your only blood kin, but you confessed yourself that he never did anything but torment and manipulate you. Do not cry for a brute like him. You are well rid of him, I promise you."

She shook her head, turning to gaze at Sir Balduin with widened eyes. Did he truly not understand? "I did not mean Serafino."

He looked puzzled for a moment, then horror fell over his face. "Vincenzo? You still weep for him?"

Lucianna had learned to recognize jealousy when men had begun to swarm around Siri and vie for her favor at the tender age of thirteen. Jealousy was clearly the look that accompanied Sir Balduin's horror, but she could not comprehend how that was possible.

It could not be. She banished the nonsensical thought with another sharp shake of her head. "Do I look like a foolish girl? I dried my tears for Vincenzo twenty-nine years ago. But that does not mean I forgot the lesson he taught me and that you affirmed to me this day."

"That *I*—" Sir Balduin broke off, then gasped. "*I* did not walk out on you. Saints! Is that what you thought?"

"What else should I think? You listened to my story in crushing silence, and at the end—"

"At the end, I left to hunt down that devil brother of yours, bloody his nose, and hurl him out of Vere. Triston is not the only one capable of losing his temper, you know. Serafino is gone, and he will never bully or threaten you again."

Sir Balduin had been the one to throw Serafino out of the castle? She glanced down at his hands and saw the bluing bruises on his knuckles.

"Lucianna—" he spoke her name on a husky breath. "I know that I have disappointed you again and again. I cannot learn Italian, however hard I try. I am an abysmal poet. And apparently you are right in that I am pathetically slow to understand a woman's feelings, though to be fair, the idea that you feared I might blame you for anything your brother had said or done was too incomprehensible to cross my mind." He hesitated. "I believe that you still love me . . . ?"

He trailed off with the faintest question in his voice. Slow-witted, indeed, to wonder after the way she had kissed him earlier. She tried to speak, but found her lungs suspended by what he might say next, so she merely nodded.

He expelled a breath that might have been relief, but the lines in his face remained tense and anxious. "Yet in spite of that, I know how you have longed for your home in Venice. If you still wish to return there after Siri's baby is born, I will not ask you again to stay. But I will not lie to you. I wish a thousand times over that you would remain and marry me instead."

She searched his eyes, remembering the way they had blazed at the end of her recital of her past. "How can you wish that? I am not a lady. I am not even a merchant's daughter. I am—"

He set a finger to her lips, then cupped her face between his hands. "How did Lady Siri say it? 'You are my own dear Lucianna.' How could you think any of the rest would have mattered to me?"

"It mattered to Vincenzo." Her voice came out small, wary. If she had ceased to weep for him, the cut of his scorn had never faded. "He could not flee from me fast enough when he learned of my birth."

"I am not a vain, selfish boy, too blind to recognize the worth of a priceless pearl. Lucianna." He repeated her name, a warm caress of confidence now on his lips. "The nuns christened you most aptly. I thought myself resigned to slipping quietly into the winter of my life, until you came and brought me back the light of spring."

"Not spring," she said on a sigh. "I, too, am in the autumn of my years."

"Two autumn hearts," he murmured. His arms slid to encircle her waist. "But confess. When we kiss, it feels like spring again."

She could not deny it, going so far as to giggle like a guilty girl when he bent to nuzzle her ear.

But she said, "What about *Don* Triston? Was he not furious when you told him about me?"

"I have not told him yet," Sir Balduin replied, pressing a kiss to her forehead. "But when I do, you do not need to fear. He will be the last man to judge you for the sins of your kin. Have you forgotten how his own father died beneath the cloud of suspected treason to the crown?"

Under Serafino's masterful manipulation, Lucianna had indeed allowed herself to forget Triston's dark past. Triston had a turbulent temper, but she knew he was not a hypocrite. Perhaps Serafino truly had made her fear for nothing.

She felt a movement against the small of her back and craned her neck to try to see what Sir Balduin was doing. He revealed the answer by finding her hand and sliding his emerald ring onto her finger.

"We are agreed, then," he said with such cheerfulness that it emphatically swept away her lingering doubts. "You will cease the Italian lessons to please me, and you may chide me to your heart's content when I forget to be home for dinner. I may shower you will silver needles if I wish to do so, and I shall spare your ears any more of my frightful songs."

"But you have a very handsome voice," she protested. "It should please me to hear you sing again. Only do not say my hair is foxy or that I have a milky smile."

"Never!" he vowed. "Then the marriage bargain is struck. Now all we have left to do is to wed."

"But Serafino—" joy squeezed out of her as she spoke his name. "You do not know him. He will come back when he learns we have married, he will demand that we pay him to keep quiet or he will spread my shameful birth far and wide. You will be humiliated among all who know you." She broke away from him. Serafino would haunt her forever unless she stood firm against Sir Balduin's temptations. "I will not let that happen, nor will I let you pay him a single *denaro* for my sake! *No!* I would sooner return to Venice and never lay eyes on you again then let him take such vile advantage of you."

Sir Balduin threw back his head and laughed. "Ah, there is my tigress-love. Always seeking to protect first those you care for." He paused and drew a husky breath. "And how I thank the Saints that you count me among their number."

He caught her back into his arms despite her attempt at resistance and kissed her so long and lingeringly that her knees went week.

"We shall not see that black sheep brother of yours again," he promised. "I only wish you had trusted me to blacken his eyes the day he rode into the bailey. He knows that is what awaits him if he ever returns to Poitou."

She stared suspiciously at his tone. "You said you only bloodied his nose."

"I assure you, it bled quite copiously when I broke it. And his eyes offended me, so I hit those, too. The villain had no right to eyes as beautiful as yours. Bah! as Perrin would say. I find the entire subject of your brother distasteful. I insist on one more clause to our marriage bargain: we will never speak of him again."

Lucianna gave a small, disatisfied *hmph*. "That is three clauses for you and only two for me."

"Then name a third, my tigress-love."

She thought a moment, then blushed and hid her face against his breast. "I shall name it on our wedding night."

IV

The home of Walter Geraud ~ Venice 1155

*L*ucianna silently suppressed the pang in her heart as she laid the child in its father's arms. She was happy for Elisabetta. Nay, she was joyful! Two years ago a healthy boy, and now a beautiful, vigorous daughter, judging from the power of her lungs as she had wailed for her first meal. Now sated and content, she slept cradled in Walter Geraud's embrace as he carried his new daughter into the light of the window to view her in the spring morning's light.

Fingers fluttered against Lucianna's, drawing her attention back to the mother. Elisabetta's dark hair spilled over the pillows and streamed across the blankets of the wide bed, the strands still tangled and damp with the exertions of giving birth. Lucianna saw Elisabetta's flushed cheeks and wrung out the compress floating in the basin of water on the nearby table, then with a tender motion wiped her friend's moist brow.

"You will take care of them," Elisabetta murmured, her lids seeking to close in weariness from the birthing. "If anything happens — "

"Nothing will happen," Lucianna chided. "You were the same after Simon was born. Three days of fever and chills, then perfectly well again."

Simon, now Siriol. French names to please her husband. Lucianna did not approve, but Walter had been generous to take her in when he married Elisabetta, so she tried not to meddle between them. It was not always easy, for Walter was a man and men had many silly

160

notions of life. Worse, he was a foreigner hailing from the county of Poitou near France, and had proven deplorably slow to learn Italian. Lucianna had never thought to be grateful for the French she learned in the convent, but thanks to Elisabetta's stubborn insistence that she share her lessons all those years ago, she never found herself shut out of any conversation between husband and wife.

"You are right," Elisabetta said with that smile Lucianna could always hear in her voice. It curved slowly across Elisabetta's lips as well. "I worry for nothing. I think it may be the way of mothers, for I have worried ever so much since my babes were born. Do you think she is pretty?"

Lucianna did not need to ask whom she meant. "I have never seen a more beautiful babe, except perhaps for Simon."

Elisabetta laughed aloud at that, for she knew Lucianna said it to please her. It was true, though. Two-year-old Simon was as golden and handsome as his father, and though it was too soon to judge little Siriol's complexion, Lucianna feared the babe's father's blood would overwhelm her mother's again.

Elisabetta shifted restlessly in the bed. Lucianna instinctively knew her need as always, and arranged another pillow behind her back to prop her further up. It had been the same after Simon's birth. Tired as she was, Elisabetta fought her exhaustion to stay awake and gaze upon her daughter and her husband.

"You are right," Elisabetta repeated. "We shall have many years together yet, all of us. But someday . . . someday it will be only you and Simon and Siriol. And when that day comes, I shall not be afraid, for I know you will love them as I do."

"Hush." Such talk as this made Lucianna cross. Elisabetta had spoken the same after Simon was born.

Elisabetta insisted now, as she had then, "Some things I know, Lucianna. I do not know how, but I know it of a certainty. You will love my children with that fierce, protective heart of yours. And someday, you will be loved, too."

Lucianna shook her head. "I am content to be your sister and their aunt. Do not tease me with what cannot be."

"It can be. You are only nineteen and you still have your dowry."

Lucianna turned her head to also watch the father and the babe.
"Lucianna?"

Lucianna bit the inside of her lip, hoping Elisabetta would not
observe the slight motion. But her silence betrayed her.

"You do not have it?" Elisabetta lowered her voice to a hiss so
that her husband could not overhear. "Do not tell me you gave it to
Serafino!"

"Of course not. But I have no need of it. I do not wish to wed. I
have all the family I will ever need here with you and Walter."

"That is nonsense. You are young and pretty and men still look
at you with desire, however haughty and proud you treat them.
What happened to your dowry if you did not throw it away on your
worthless brother?"

"I used it to buy some white samite for Simon's baptismal
gown, and now for Siriol's. It is a very expensive cloth."

"With silver threads, which you further embellished with
exquisite white embroidery for Simon's gown. But Walter said he
bought the cloth with a costly commission to illuminate a Book of
Hours."

"The commission was true, but I told him to keep the money for
I wished to give a gift to his son, and now to his daughter. And I told
him not to tell you, for I knew how it would displease you. I have a
few coins left, but not enough to win a husband. So there is no more
reason for you to importune me to look at this man or that." She met
Elisabetta's dark, unhappy eyes. "It can be no other way, you know
it. Serafino would never let me marry in peace."

Elisabetta stretched out a hand. Lucianna took it in hers, relieved
to feel the flush of heat already faded from Elisabetta's slim fingers.

"Lucianna," Elisabetta said, her voice soft but very firm, "I did
not question your dream in the convent, did I?"

"No. But it was a false dream."

Elisabetta's teeth openly fretted her lower lip for a moment.
"Perhaps," she said at last. "Or perhaps you did not understand it.
Perhaps it was your grandfather's name. We never asked Serafino,
did we?"

"No, and I do not wish to know, for if it was, he was either father to a thief or to a woman who did not want me."

Elisabetta squeezed Lucianna's fingers, imparting understanding. Lucianna knew she would say no more of the dream.

"But some things I know," Elisabetta insisted. "I knew while I carried him that my first babe would be a boy, and I knew that Siriol would be a girl. I told you that before their birth, and was I not right?"

Lucianna reluctantly admitted that she had been.

"And the way I knew, the feeling of certainty that came upon me with my babes — it is the same that came upon me when you wept in my arms after Vincenzo left you. I do not know when or how, but someday, someone who does not care about dowries or wicked fathers or unscrupulous brothers will love and cherish you. I pray I will live to see it proved to you, but if I do not, I know it will happen all the same."

Lucianna leaned down to embrace Elisabetta, unconvinced, but tears stinging at her eyes for the strength of her friend's love.

"All that matters to me," Lucianna said, "is that whatever comes to us both, we will share it always as sisters."

She kissed Elisabetta as a footstep brought Walter and the babe back to the bed.

"You two have cozed for a very long time," Walter said with a grin, "but it is my turn to sit awhile with my wife. Someone should tell Simon that he has a new sister."

Lucianna straightened, whisking away her tears, praying that Walter had not seen, but he turned after placing the babe in her mother's arms and startled Lucianna by kissing her on the cheek.

"Oh!" Lucianna exclaimed, her face warming in confusion.

Walter laughed. "I know that most days I vex you as much as you vex me, but this house would be a dull place without you, Lucianna. I could not ask a truer friend to my wife or more tender aunt to my children. Thank you."

Blushing, disconcerted, but entirely content, Lucianna slipped from the room and left the parents alone with their new baby daughter.

Epilogue

Vere Castle, Poitou
Four months later

Lucianna remembered the words as if they had fallen on her ears only yesterday. *Someday, someone who does not care about dowries or wicked fathers or unscrupulous brothers will love and cherish you.* She did not know how Elisabetta had known it, but after all these years, Sir Balduin de Soler had finally made her dear friend's promise come true.

She smiled at the tiny fingers that wound around her thumb. She could not seem to calm the fluttering of her heart. It had been a very long time since she had held a babe— twenty-five years, in fact, when she had cradled Siri in her arms. It thrilled her that she had not forgotten how to rock her body to still an infant's cries, or how to kiss the rosy cheeks to win a tiny chortle, or hum a tune that made the wee eyes softly close in sleep.

"She is your image, *carissima*," Lucianna murmured.

Siri yawned and stretched, arching her back from where she sat in her illuminating chair in her workshop. Perrin had begged her to resume his painting lessons, whining that it had been three whole months since his sister had been born. But Siri had spent so much time yawning and struggling to hold her eyes open, that Perrin had finally wandered away from the desk to study his new sibling.

"She is very loud," he pronounced. "I can hear her crying at night all the way in my bedchamber."

"Then imagine how Lady Siri must feel with the babe's cradle right beside her bed. It is no wonder she is half asleep. I should not have let you plague her into taking up her paints. Go away," Lucianna said, "and let me put her and your sister back to bed."

There was a time when Lucianna's curt rebukes had intimidated the boy, but he had grown regrettably impervious to them as his precociousness had coaxed a maternal affection in her and softened the force, if not the frequency, of her chastisements.

"Can't you leave the baby?" he said. "I can watch her while you take Siri away to sleep. I need to study her to understand why you keep saying she looks like Siri. Because I don't see it. She just looks fat and pink to me, and Siri isn't either anymore."

Siri trilled with laughter from her chair. "Thank you, Perrin. I am not as slender as I was when I married your Papa, but I am trying very hard to restrain my craving for sweets." She slid from the chair and came to stand beside Lucianna and the babe. "You think she looks like me?"

"She will be your image," Lucianna repeated. "Well, nearly so. I am certain eyes as blue as hers will remain unchanged. She has your little nose and your round, rosy cheeks, and I am sure her hair will come in fair."

She sat down on a bench near the window and permitted Perrin to run a light finger over the baby's head.

"There's hardly any there," he said. "You can't even see it, you can only feel a little fuzz."

"*Si*, and that fuzz would be dark, not white, if she was meant to have your papa's black curls." Lucianna was certain of it. She tilted her head in consideration. "But she will have Triston's stubborn chin, I think."

Sir Balduin had been right. Triston had waved away any association of guilt between Lucianna and Serafino, remarking that however regrettable the consequences, one could not control the choices of one's kin, even when that kin's actions brought dour repercussions down upon their families. Lucianna had pledged to herself never to criticize Triston again, a vow that would be easy to keep once she and Sir Balduin moved to Dauvillier Castle.

The baby gave a little gurgling sigh and snuggled deeper into Lucianna's arms. Another quiver wove through her. She wondered if Siri saw it.

"What shall I call her when she grows up?" Perrin asked. "Elisabetta or Isabelle?"

"Elisabetta," Lucianna said firmly, but a strong voice from the doorway contradicted her.

"Isabelle. Here in Poitou, at least."

Despite her new pledge, Lucianna sent a challenging glower at Triston as he entered the room with her husband. Then she caught Sir Balduin's glance at the babe before his gaze lifted to hers.

Siri comforted Lucianna with a tender smile. "It is all right. You and I shall call her Elisabetta."

She bent down to kiss Lucianna on the cheek just as Sir Balduin's grin brought a rush of warmth to Lucianna's face.

Siri startled away, laid an anxious hand to Lucianna's brow, then appeared to catch her mistake. She laughed again. "Oh, you are only blushing." Her jewel-blue eyes narrowed. "Why are you blushing?"

The question so heated Lucianna's cheeks that she knew they must be scarlet. Sir Balduin did not help matters by glowing so proudly as he strolled across the room to her side that she knew he must either blurt out their secret or burst.

"Shall you tell them, or shall I?" he asked his wife, leaning over to tickle a finger beneath the baby's chin, provoking

Elisabetta into stirring with something very like a sleepy chuckle.

"It—it is the silliest thing, *carissima*," Lucianna stammered. "At my age—! I was sure it was only a jest when I made my husband swear to the third clause of our marriage bargain."

She remembered how drowsily he had done so, holding her fast in his embrace, her ear nestled against his beating heart as they had drifted asleep together in the soft afterglow of love.

Triston joined the circle around his new daughter. "Your marriage bargain?" he asked. He looked only half-alert to an answer, watching in a thoroughly besotted manner as Elisabetta stretched and waved her little arms.

But Lucianna saw that Siri now stood wide awake with a mischievous smile twitching across her lips.

"You told me about the other clauses," Siri said. "The needles and the nagging and the singing and the cessation of the Italian lessons, and *all* of us are glad for the vow never to speak Serafi—" She slapped her hand to her mouth, but the sapphire eyes danced merrily. "I mean your brother's name again. Three promises from you and two from Sir Balduin. I did not think it like you to agree to stand so uneven in the marriage. What is this mysterious third promise Sir Balduin made?"

She scooped Elisabetta out of Lucianna's arms, ignoring Lucianna's protest, and handed their daughter to Triston.

Lucianna sprang up from her chair, hiding her embarrassment by scolding Triston for waking the babe as Sir Balduin announced far too loudly, "To name our firstborn son Panfilo."

Triston looked so startled he nearly dropped Elisabetta. Lucianna squealed and caught the infant back to her own embrace.

"You are having a baby?" Triston exclaimed to Sir Balduin.

"*I* am having a baby," Lucianna snapped. "Now look what you have done!"

Elisabetta had begun to wail, which turned into an earsplitting keen when Siri flung her arms around both her and Lucianna in a fearsome hug.

"Be careful, *carissima*," Lucianna chided.

"Oh, she is fine," Siri said. "She is amazingly sturdy." But she took Elisabetta and bounced her gently against her shoulder until the keening turned to charming hiccups. "Lucianna, I cannot tell you how happy I am for you! But what if it is a daughter?"

Perrin piped up. "If it is, she can call her Elisabetta. Then we can call this one Isabelle and I shan't have to be confused."

Lucianna feigned indifference. "If it is daughter, then my husband may choose." But she remembered her dream of so long ago. She thought Serafino had destroyed it, but perhaps this had been its meaning all along? Not a father, but a son. She moved her hand protectively, caressingly to the growing life inside her, and saw Siri smile with her.

"Panfilo?" Triston said to Sir Balduin. "You agreed to that?"

Siri's smile vanished. "Cosimo would have been a perfectly good name for a boy, and there is nothing wrong with Panfilo." Her tartness revealed that the mood swings preceding Elisabetta's birth had not entirely subsided.

Sir Balduin's shoulders half-lifted in a shrug. He caught Lucianna's glare and swiftly resumed his normal posture. "I am a man of my word," he said, "and I gave it to her with all my love."

He crossed the room to take his wife's hands and gaze deeply into her eyes. He paraphrased the words he had said to her when her past reared up again the day before their wedding, dismaying her at what name she should give the priest on the morrow.

"She came into this home as Lucianna Fabio, it was Lucianna Fabio I married, and," he added with the insight neither of them had possessed that day, "it is Lucianna Fabio's father we will honor at our son's birth."

An illusion, perhaps, conjured by a lost, lonely girl in an

abbey, but one that had brought her incomprehensible comfort before Serafino. Sir Balduin had convinced her with that tenderness he only exposed to her that it would bring the heavens joy to wrap her in that comfort again. Now heaven had set the seal on his words with a child.

Her hands shifted nervously within her husband's grasp, betraying the worry that recurred with disquieting frequency through her shining bouts of happiness. "You do not think I am too old to be a mother?" she asked.

Siri *hrmphed* her opinion of Lucianna's fear, while Sir Balduin said, "No more than I am too old to be a father. We will find our way through parenthood together."

He paused as Perrin begged Siri to sit down in her chair by the desk and show him the baby again. When Siri obliged and Triston moved away to join them, Sir Balduin drew Lucianna close to him and kissed her. Then he nuzzled her ear until she thought she might suffocate from smothering her giggles.

"Old," he scoffed softly. "You and I?" His eyes twinkled down at her. "This child will keep us rooted in spring for a very long time."

No two persons ever read the same book

The great writer Edmund Wilson once said, "No two persons ever read the same book."

I suppose in the same way, no two persons ever see quite the same flower or the identical cloud in the sky or even taste a cookie exactly the same way. That is what makes each of us unique.

What book did *you* just read? Would you be so kind as to take just a minute or two to write a review of *Loving Lucianna* and share with others what made this story unique for *you*?

Lucianna, Sir Balduin, and their author will thank you!

Italian Glossary

Most of these words are defined within the story, but a few of them are not, so here is a list of definitions:

Ahimè! – alas!

Amici – friends

Amore – love, darling

Bambino, bambina – baby

Bella – beautiful, lovely

Buongiorno – good morning; good day

Bugiarda – liar

Cara – dear one

Cara amica - cherished friend

Carissima – dearest, most loved or cherished

Che diavolo! – What the devil!

Cognato – brothers-in-law

Convento – convent

Denaro, denari (plural) – small silver coin used in medieval Venice

Don – lord

Donna – lady

Finale – final

Fratello - brother

Grazie – thank you

Imbecille - imbecile

Infine – at last

La forsa – police force in Venice

Ladro, ladra - thief

Maiale – pig

Matrone – matrons

Mia, mio – my

No – no

Non più – no more

Paffuto – chubby, plump

Pazienza – patient

Pazzi – madmen

Piazza – square

Santa Caterina – Saint Catherine

Scusi – excuse me

Sempre – always

Si – yes

Signora – form of address for a married woman

Signore (Signor when appears before a proper name) – sir; form of address for a man

Signorina, signorine (plural) – form of address for single women and young ladies

Sorella, sorelle (plural) – sister

Sta provando imbrogliarci – He is trying to cheat us

Storia d'amore – love affair

Uomo avido – greedy man

Veramente – truly

Glossary of Medieval Terms

Almonry – the almshouse of a religious order where nuns or monks dispensed alms (money, food, clothes, etc.) to the poor; sometimes included rooms where poor children were housed, fed and clothed

Bailey – the courtyard of a castle

Castellan – governor of a castle; since a baron or knight might hold multiple castles from the king and could not personally manage all of them at once, he often assigned a "castellan" to administer a castle in his absence.

Cendal – a fabric made of silk

Crenellated – a wall possessing both crenels (open spaces) and merlons (solid portions of the wall between the spaces)

Dais – a raised platform in the castle **hall**

Dinner – the midday meal, usually taking place between 12 – 2 PM

Dowry – just as women were expected to bring a dowry (some money or land) into a secular marriage, similarly women who desired to become nuns (who were known as brides of Christ) were expected to bring a dowry of money or land when they entered a convent

Fortnight – two weeks (from "fourteen nights")

Girdle – a belt worn around the waist

Illumination/illuminating – the art of decorating books in the Middle Ages with miniatures or ornamental designs painted in brilliant colors or silver or gold leaf to "illuminate" or bring light to the pages

Jongleur – an itinerate entertainer in medieval France and England proficient in juggling and acrobatics, as well as in music

Keep – the main tower and central residence area of a castle

Mead – a medieval garden designed to imitate a small meadow

Oblate – a child "donated" to a monastery or convent by his or her parents to be brought up in the religious life

Parchment – material made from animal skin used for the pages of books or other writing

Poitiers – capital of **Poitou**

Poitou – a region of west-central France ruled by Henry II of England during the Middle Ages

Psaltery – a book containing the Book of Psalms from the Bible

Samite – a heavy silk fabric, sometimes with interwoven with silver or gold threads

Squire – a boy between the ages of 14 and 20 in training to become a knight; a squire might be knighted at the age of 21, although some men never advanced to knighthood and remained squires all their lives

Surcote – also known as the surcoat or super-tunic; a secondary **tunic** worn over an under **tunic**, usually more elaborately decorated

The hall or great hall – the central living space of the castle inside the **keep**; the ceremonial and legal center

Trencher – large slice of stale bread, cut either round or square, and used as "plates" for medieval dining

Troubadour – a class of medieval poets who flourished in modern-day southern France known as Occitania (included Poitou and Aquitaine) between 1100-1350

Tunic – a sleeved, loose fitting outer garment worn by both men and women; could be worn alone or under a **surcote**; for the man could be knee or ankle length

Author's Note

Loving Lucianna is based on some characters who originated in my earlier medieval romance, *Illuminations of the Heart*. Although *Illuminations of the Heart* was originally published in 2009, the first draft was actually written much earlier. Emailing was just beginning to come into vogue, and search engines like Yahoo and Google were still a considerable way out on the horizon. When it came time for me to choose some Italian names for the story, I simply picked a few names I liked—Lucianna and Elisabetta in particular—from a book of names I had tucked away in my hardcover research library. It was so long ago, I can't even recall where I came up with the surnames Fabio and Gallo.

Fast forward to 2014 and my decision to write a novella about Lucianna and Sir Balduin. While I was mulling over plot ideas for their story, it popped into my mind that Lucianna had a black sheep brother who we never met in *Illuminations of the Heart*. The first question became what to name him. And the first answer that occurred to me was the name of a black sheep ancestor of mine who my sister (the genealogist in the family) had discovered in the interim between my two writing projects. His name was Serafino Amorosi (sometimes spelled Amoroso). Fortunately for us, if not for him, he left behind a court record describing his misdeeds, which included theft of "a rifle, some silver, and a few other objects (including a frying pan!)" and assault "which left great wounds on the victims." (See transcript that follows.)

Including a Serafino Amorosi in my story (although born many years before my ancestor) seemed too good an opportunity to pass up. After all, where's the fun in writing a story if an author can't include a few inside family jokes?

Having determined to give Serafino a starring role in my new novella, I found myself seized with the spirit of family history. In 2014 the internet has become almost as much a part of our daily lives as waking up in the morning (for those who manage to turn it off long enough to go to bed). The family history information my sister once compiled by hand she now regularly uploads to a family history internet site called FamilySearch (www.familysearch.org). This time instead of restricting myself to names in my research library each time I needed a new Italian name for *Loving Lucianna*, I turned instead to my family tree. I called up the family "fan chart" on FamilySearch and plucked off names for new characters.

It occurred to me, however, that except for Serafino, who came to a rather bad end and thus had not much excuse to complain of the way I used his name, my other ancestors might or might not be excited about being included in my story (since some played more positive roles than others). So just to be safe, in case I meet them someday on the "other side," I decided to mix and match first and last names, so that aside from Serafino Amorosi, no direct link exists between the names in this story and my ancestors. However, for the curious, here are the names in the book that came from my family tree.

First names:
Agata

Antonia
Domenico
Giovanni
Maria Angela
Panfilo
Rosaria
Serafino
Vincenzo

Surnames:
Amorosi
d'Arro
Mirolli
Piccoli
Venanzio

Abruzzo, the area of Italy where my grandmother's family came from, also got a mention in the story. And, after much wrestling with the plot, so did the notorious frying pan. (See reference to "frying pan" in the transcript that follows. I couldn't resist trying to include it. I mean, really, who breaks into a windmill and steals a frying pan?)

All other names and combinations of names in this story are fictional.

Summary of document about Serafino Amorosi included with his daughters' 1824 marriage documents

Summary of document about Serafino Amorosi included with his daughters' 1824 marriage documents

(from microfilm #1384893, Family History Library of the Church of Jesus Christ of Latter-day Saints, Salt Lake City, UT)

Translated for my sister, Janet DiPastena, by Mary Weaver, a colleague at the Family History Library.

27 June 1816
Special Court

Accusation of Serafino Amorosi, son of Giuseppe, who is dead, of the town of Torricella, age 45, an ironworker; and Domenico Rocchio, son of Vincenzo, age 25, of the town of Gesso, a farmer. These two broke into the houses of two people, beat them up and wounded them. They were sentenced to perpetual forced labor.

Details of the accusations against Serafino and Domenico:

On the evening of December 16, 1815, Serafino Amoroso, Domenico Rocchio, Domenico Madonna, Ubaldo Colarelli, and one other went to a windmill in the territory of Fallascoso. The first two had a musket and a bayonet. The windmill belongs to Vincenzo di Stefano. Using a ladder, they climbed in and stole two lamps, a frying pan, and a wool jacket. Having performed this stealthy act, this band of aggressors went the same night to a rural house near Gesso inhabited by the priest Don Giovanni Pellicciotta.

They planned to commit another assault, using violence to complete the act, in order to get a lot of money. During this effort of the group, two of the group, Serafino and one other not yet apprehended, went into the house, while the others stayed outside, waiting. These two, having gone in with the musket, beat up the priest and his two housemen. The people in the house were left with multiple wounds.

They stole a rifle, some silver, and a few other objects. Not having found any money, they threatened the priest at the cost of his life, forcing him to write a letter to his brother, who is staying in Gesso, telling him to send 200,000 coins in a money bag. They forced one of the servants to take the letter to the person it was directed to. They tied up the priest and took him to a solitary place, holding him sequestered until the return of the servant. They also formed other plans.

The priest, after having written this letter by force, was left near a window. While the two thieves were distracted getting the servant out the door, the priest noticed he wasn't being watched. He threw himself out the window, which was near the ground. He then ran with all his might, coming to another house nearby.

The aggressors were disappointed by the escape of the priest. They thought of nothing but getting away. They took the rifle, silver, and other objects. The house where the priest went was attached to the priest's house and belongs to the servants. No one lives in the windmill where the first crime was committed.

Domenico Madonna and Ubaldo Colarelli were arrested a few days later. They stated in court that Serafino Amoroso, Domenico Rocchio, and one other were the ones who performed the crime. They also explained the surrounded circumstances. All of the above information came from their statements. They confessed and were condemned on May 22.

Amoroso and Rocchio rebutted totally those statements, saying they are false, and that Colarelli and Madonna said this to spite them. However, in spite of their assertions, they haven't been able to prove whatsoever that Colarelli and Madonna had iniquitous desires to slander them or that they wanted to destroy their reputations. In fact, it has been noticed to the contrary, that Colarelli is a relative of Amoroso's, having taken as a wife a daughter of Amoroso's. These are the facts.

The court considering the confessions of Colarelli and Madonna, recognized Amoroso and Rocchio as the accused. The statements of Colarelli and Madonna were considered as entirely true, resulting in the other two being condemned as guilty of the misdeeds. There has been no argument to make the judges doubt, even a little, the veracity of those statements previously proclaimed and accepted. The court declares Serafino Amoroso and Domenico Rocchio guilty, 1st of an attack on the two houses, stealing a frying pan and other objects from Vincenzo di Stefano, committed at night by five people, armed and with ladders; and 2nd, the theft of a rifle, silver, and other objects from don Giovanni Pellicciotta of Gesso, also committed at night by five people with arms and violence, which left great wounds on the victims.

The court considers that the first robbery requires forced labor for a period of time, and the second deserves forced labor perpetually, based on Criminal Code #384 and #382. The court condemns Serafino Amoroso and Domenico Rocchio to forced labor for life. They are also fined a sum of money for court costs, but this does not cover damages for the victims. That will be handled in civil court.

Discussion Questions

~ Triston refers to Lucianna as a "complicated" and "difficult" woman. What aspects of Lucianna's character did you find difficult to relate to? What aspects of her character did you sympathize with?

~ *Loving Lucianna* takes place in two locations, medieval Venice and medieval Poitou. Did the author succeed in giving a different flavor to each of these locations? If so, how? If not, how did they feel the same?

~ How did you feel about the flashback scenes to Venice? Did they enhance or distract from the rest of the story, and how did they do so? How did Lucianna's experiences in these scenes shape the woman she later became?

~ How did you feel about the relationship between Lucianna and Elisabetta? Did it feel authentic? Did you agree with all the decisions these two young women made? Why or why not? What decisions might you have made differently? How would your decisions have changed the course of the story?

~ Have you ever had a friendship with someone as close as the friendship between Lucianna and Elisabetta? How did that friendship affect your life?

~ What were your feelings about Sir Balduin? Do you feel he should have stood up to Lucianna more? How do you think she would have reacted?

~ Why do you think the author chose the title *Loving Lucianna* for this story? How did other characters show their love for Lucianna? How did Lucianna show her love for other characters in this book?

~ What are some things you learned about the medieval time period while you read? Do you think it's important to learn about other time periods than our own? Why or why not?

~ Were you satisfied with the ending? If so, why? If not, how would you like the story to have ended?

Join my Medieval World!

Sign up for Joyce's newsletter to receive announcements on new releases, special promotions and offers, participate in monthly giveaways, get subscriber-only glimpses into writing updates, book recommendations, historical trivia, and more! You are free to unsubscribe at any time.

Sign up at joycedipastena.com

Acknowledgments

My heartfelt thanks go to my wonderful beta readers ~ (first round) Sara Acevedo, Brittany Gardner, Donna Hatch, Stacy Johnson, Laura Miller, Melissa Pitney, Kaitlyn Shiflet, Jordan Thomas, Julie Wallace, and (second round) Kurt Kammeyer, Wanda Luce, Melanie Mason, Heidi Murphy, and Marilyn Rigby ~ each of whom added valuable insights to various versions of this story, making it possible for me to continually improve each round of revisions.

Thanks also to my editor, Nancy Campbell Allen, for giving this manuscript its final polish.

And last but far from least, to my sister, Janet DiPastena, whose love for family history provided me with so many wonderful names for this story.

About the Author

Joyce DiPastena dreamed of green medieval forests while growing up in the dusty copper mining town of Kearny, Arizona. She filled her medieval hunger by reading the books of Thomas B. Costain (where she fell in love with King Henry II of England), and later by attending the University of Arizona where she graduated with a degree in history, specializing in the Middle Ages.

When she's not writing, Joyce loves to read, play the piano, eat chocolate, and spend time with her sister and friends. A highlight of her year is attending the annual Arizona Renaissance Festival.

Joyce is a multi-published, multi-award winning author who specializes in sweet medieval romances heavily spiced with mystery and adventure. She lives with her two cats, Nyxie and Calypso, in Mesa, Arizona.

Email her at joyce@joycedipastena.com.

Visit her website at joycedipastena.com.